WITHDRAWN

the
doomsdaybox

lzer & Bray is an imprint of HarperCollins Publishers.

The Doomsday Box: A Shadow Project Adventure
Copyright © 2011 by Herbie Brennan

r information address HarperCollins Children's Books, a division of
Collins Publishers, 10 East 53rd Street, New York, NY 10022.
www.harpercollinschildrens.com

Library of Congress Cataloging-in-Publication Data

box : a Shadow Project adventure / by Herbie Brennan. —

king on a highly classified espionage project, four
s go back in time to the Cold War in 1962 to prevent a
of the bubonic plague in the twenty-first century.
5-175647-4 (trade bdg.)
on. 2. Plague—Fiction. 3. Cold War—Fiction. 4. Time
5. Extrasensory perception—Fiction. 6. Astral
ion. 7. England—Fiction.] I. Title.
2011   2010015947

Typography by Carla Weise
14   15   LP/RRDB   10 9 8 7 6 5 4 3 2 1
❖
First Edition

the
doom

a shado

her

Brennan, Herbie
  The doomsday
1st ed.
    p.   cm.
  Summary: Wo
English teenage
global outbreak
  ISBN 978-0-0
  [1. Spies—Fict
travel—Fiction.
projection—Fic
PZ7.B75153Doo
[Fic]—dc22

BA

An Imprint

11   12   13

For James and Penny with much love

Opal, London, England

Opal fastened the strap around her ankle and stood up to admire her new shoes. The school uniform didn't help—that frumpy pleated skirt!—but at least she could get an idea. She grinned at the image in the mirror. Fab shoes: no doubt about that. Very red, very high heels (would she actually be able to walk in them?), and those crisscross straps were something else. Her father would have a fit!

On the other hand, her girl friends would be green with envy.

"Walk up and down a bit—get the feel," the assistant suggested. "Don't just look in the mirror."

Opal did as she was told, teetering a little. "I'm not used to high heels," she said apologetically. The Project frowned on high heels.

"They do take some getting used to," said the assistant, as if he had personal experience. "But they suit you,

1

dear. Stand by the mirror and put one foot ahead of the other like a model. That's right. . . . Oooh, you've set me all aquiver!"

They were hideously expensive, something else her father would go mad about, even though Opal was going to buy them with her own money from the Project. She *deserved* nice shoes. The Project was hard work—dangerous too—and she *still* had to find time for school. She *definitely* deserved nice shoes.

She left the shop in her old flat black pumps (regulation school issue, along with the pleated skirt), but the box in the bag seemed to be calling out to her, singing a little tune. *New* shoes, *high* heels, red, and *absolutely perfect* whatever her father was going to say. She wondered if she dared wear them at the Project. (There was no official dress code, of course—most of the operatives slopped around in jeans and sweaters, except for her father, who always wore a suit, and Mr. Carradine, who sometimes did.) That would liven up the office. She could just see her father's face. Not that she would be wearing the outfit for her father—really, secretly, she would be wearing it for Michael.

She could imagine his face too, probably just as shocked as her father's. He was cute—boy, was he cute!—but he was just the tiniest bit uptight about some things. She didn't know why she went out with him sometimes.

Well, she did, but he could afford to loosen up a little.

Opal glanced in the window of the shop she'd just left. They were featuring a pair of shoes in green that were quite nice. Maybe she would have been better off buying *them*. She thought about it for a nanosecond, then moved away. Maybe Topshop would have something to go with the red shoes, something that would get Michael's attention.

Opal glanced at her watch. Lots of time to get to Oxford Street, especially if she took a cab. She turned left, heading for the taxi stand, when somebody grabbed her from behind.

She was so surprised, she didn't even think to scream.

[2]

Opal, the Shadow Project, outside London

Opal felt like screaming at her father. There was a strange girl in the office, a peculiar creature with pale skin and pale eyes and pale hair, wearing the oddest clothes. Danny, the newest member of the Project, was sitting beside her, a bemused look on his face. But the worst thing of all was that Michael was there, looking very cool in sweater and jeans while she, Opal, was humiliated within an inch of her life in her *school uniform*!

And actually, that wasn't the worst thing of all. The worst thing of all was that her father didn't even seem to notice her fury. "Is your passport up-to-date?" he asked her, frowning slightly.

"Your people practically snatched me off the street," Opal snapped. "I thought I was being *kidnapped*!"

"It was rather urgent, I'm afraid," Sir Roland told her mildly. He raised an interrogatory eyebrow. "Passport up-to-date?"

"I don't have one," Danny remarked, more or less to himself, "on account of not being part of the jet set."

Sir Roland took an envelope from a drawer and threw it casually across his desk. "Yours has been arranged."

Danny opened the envelope and shook out a brand-new burgundy passport, gold-embossed with the United Kingdom's lion-and-unicorn coat of arms. "Shouldn't I have signed something for this?" He casually flipped it open. "Oh," he said, disappointed. "It's in my own name. Thought I might be going as James Bond."

"Going where?" Opal demanded. She caught her father's expression and added crossly, "My passport's up-to-date." As was his, if he was going with them. She had looked after all that sort of thing since her mother died.

"New York," Michael said.

Michael always seemed to be one step ahead. Her own father ran the Shadow Project, and *still* Michael seemed to know everything before she did. What was happening in New York that was so urgent she didn't have time to change before they told her about it? And who was the pale girl?

As if reading her thoughts, Sir Roland said, "You haven't met Fuchsia, Danny's new partner. Fuchsia, this is my daughter, Opal. Opal, this is Fuchsia Benson."

Fuchsia jumped up and skipped across the room.

"What's your birth sign?" she asked Opal as they shook hands.

Opal looked at her for a moment, taken aback. But eventually she said, "Taurus." She didn't believe in horoscopes, of course. Most Taureans didn't.

"Mine's Gemini with Moon in Cancer, so I'm supposed to be fey." Fuchsia grinned. "There's no scientific proof for astrology, but it's a great icebreaker, don't you think? Michael's a Leo—I asked him before you got here—so he's all butch and dominant." Fuchsia's grin widened and she dropped her voice to a whisper. "I asked Sir Roland too, but he wouldn't tell me."

I'll bet he wouldn't, Opal thought. She looked at Fuchsia curiously. Only teenagers could be Shadow Project operatives because they had minds that were open enough for the sort of espionage the Shadow Project did, but Fuchsia seemed an odd one. Perhaps she had special talents. Opal gently extricated herself and asked her father, "Why are we going to New York?" Actually, despite being mad at him, she thought New York might be fun. She could definitely find a red dress in New York.

"It's not New York, New York," her father said. "It's actually Montauk, New York. Gary Carradine will be going with you. He'll be here in a moment to brief you."

She'd never even heard of Montauk, New York, but

she expected all would be revealed when Mr. Carradine arrived. Which he did, almost at once, looking more like Nicolas Cage than ever, although London seemed to be getting to him, since he'd swapped his normal jacket and chinos for a safari suit. He was even wearing a tie.

"Hi," he said cheerfully, then, more formally to Opal's father, "Have you filled them in, Sir Roland?"

"I've mentioned Montauk."

"Where *is* Montauk?" Danny was never one to sit quietly through briefings.

"Southeastern tip of Long Island," Mr. Carradine told him. "It's a town with a nice beach—it's become a bit of a vacation spot these days. Population triples in the summer."

"So you're sending us on holiday?" Danny grinned. He was an East London boy with no respect at all for authority, something Opal secretly admired.

Carradine grinned back. "You could say that. It's a mission, but I think I can promise it won't be anything as dangerous as your last one."

Lives had been lost in the last one. Her father had come close to losing his. Hopefully the new mission would *definitely* not be as dangerous.

"But that doesn't mean you shouldn't take it seriously," Sir Roland put in soberly. "Your trip comes on the heels of a request from the National Security Agency."

"The *American* National Security Agency?" Michael asked, surprised.

"There is only one," Sir Roland said mildly. "You'd better tell them all about it, Gary."

Carradine perched on a corner of Sir Roland's desk, while Opal slipped into the chair next to Michael, who gave her a small, secret smile. He looked as handsome as ever. They both turned back toward Carradine.

"Before I tell you about the mission itself," Carradine was saying, "it might be useful to give you a little background—"

"This is classified information," Sir Roland interrupted. "So please bear in mind you are all signatories to the Official Secrets Act."

Which meant they could go to jail if they discussed what they were about to hear with anyone. It was typical of her father to remind them. He was very much a spy of the old school.

Mr. Carradine said, "Exactly. Thank you, Sir Roland. So . . . this story goes way back before you were born—more than half a century, in fact. Any of you ever hear of the Philadelphia Experiment?"

They looked at him blankly, then one by one shook their heads. Except Fuchsia, who said, "That's the ship they made invisible. My sister Julie says it's an urban myth."

Carradine nodded. "Very good, Fuchsia. Except it isn't *all* a myth, although some of the details have been distorted over the years. But let's start with the bit that is a myth. The story you'll find on the internet is that back in 1943, a character called Carlos Miguel Allende was standing on the deck of a freighter in Philadelphia harbor watching another ship, a military escort vessel called the USS *Eldridge*. An escort's not a particularly big ship, but it's not small either. All the same, it disappeared right before his eyes."

"Cool," Fuchsia said.

Carradine gave her a sidelong glance. "According to Allende, after fifteen minutes the *Eldridge* reappeared, and when he investigated, he found most of the crew were insane and several of them were actually fused into the structure of the ship. Later he discovered some of the sailors had come back with a weird affliction—they kept twitching in and out of our plane of existence. Two of them got into a fistfight in a Philly bar and disappeared in front of a whole roomful of witnesses before the second punch was thrown. There were even people who claimed the *Eldridge* materialized in Norfolk, Virginia, for a few minutes before vanishing in a green fog. Allende said he found out the whole mess started as a navy experiment aimed at making ships invisible . . . an experiment that went terribly wrong."

"Whozza," Danny said. He had the sort of blank look on his face that meant you couldn't tell whether he was genuinely impressed or just fooling around.

Carradine ignored him. "Most of that really *was* an urban myth, Fuchsia, including Carlos Miguel Allende—his real name was Carl Allen. But that's not to say there wasn't a grain of truth in the story. This was during the war, remember—the Second World War. America was very anxious to develop new weapons that would bring it to an end quickly. Since the late 1930s, the U.S. Navy had been funding a top secret program called Project Rainbow, which was set up to investigate the military possibilities of cloaking aircraft and ships using high-frequency electromagnetic fields. Somewhere around 1942, the scientists started to report limited successes using small-scale models. And in 1943, they ran an experiment using a full-sized ship."

"The *Eldridge?*" Michael asked.

Carradine nodded. "Carl Allen's story was accurate up to a point. The navy wasn't trying to make the ship optically invisible, just invisible to radar, like modern stealth aircraft. But they did use high-frequency electromagnetic fields, and the experiment did go wrong. The *Eldridge* didn't jump into hyperspace, of course, but many of the sailors did suffer mental impairment and had to be hospitalized. Nobody suspected it at the time, but high-frequency magnetic fields can influence the human brain. The fields generated on the *Eldridge* were so powerful they drove half the crew nuts. The navy covered it up, of course—not hard to do in wartime. They paid a few million in compensation to the sailors' families and closed down Project Rainbow. What use was radar invisibility if it drove your crew mad?"

"But they opened it up again in 1953," Sir Roland said in a cynical tone.

"Why?" Danny asked curiously.

"Yes, why?" Opal echoed. Even though her father worked for the government—even though *she* worked for the government—she didn't have to like what governments got up to.

Fuchsia said, "I bet they thought they could use high-frequency magnetic fields as a weapon. Zap the opposing army. Mad soldiers would be just as useless as mad sailors, except now they're on the other side."

"That's almost exactly right, Fuchsia," Carradine said, with undisguised surprise. "They started to wonder about using magnetic fields as a psychological warfare device—mind control, that sort of thing. But I expect the idea of zapping an opposing army occurred to them as well. Anyway, the core group of scientists approached Congress for funding—in a secret session, of course—and Congress turned them down. Apparently, a majority of congressmen thought the project was too danger-ous. A lot of them still remembered the Philadelphia Experiment, of course."

"So that finally killed it?" Michael asked.

"Not at all," said Carradine. "The scientists went direct to the military, and the Department of Defense offered funding and a decommissioned air force base at Montauk, New York, as a site for the work. This was before Montauk became a tourist center, so it was a sleepy little town that was perfect for a covert operation. And more importantly, the base had a radar installation that worked on a frequency the scientists believed could influence the human mind."

Why are we going to Montauk? Opal wondered. Mr. Carradine's story was all very interesting, but so far it seemed to have no connection with the Shadow Project. The Shadow Project was a top secret British-American espionage department that used teen spies like Michael, Danny, and herself, who were able to separate their minds from their physical bodies with a little help from Project technology. That was a long way from mind control.

Or was it? The thought occurred to her.

But Mr. Carradine was still talking. "By 1967, the Office of Naval Intelligence had become interested and so had the National Security Agency. They helped build a secret underground complex, something like this one."

He spread his hands to indicate the warren that was the Shadow Project, buried deep beneath a crumbling English manor house.

"Why did they need an underground complex, Mr. Carradine?" Michael asked.

"The fact was, the new Project Rainbow didn't confine itself to psychological research, although it was still using exceptionally powerful high-frequency electromagnetic fields. The team was conducting experiments in teleportation, parallel dimensions, and time travel."

There was absolute silence in the office for a moment. Then: *"Teleportation?"* Michael asked incredulously.

Opal, who was staring at Mr. Carradine, whispered, *"Time travel?"*

"They're interconnected," said Opal's father soberly. "As I understand the science, high-frequency electromagnetic fields can be used to bend space-time. Once you bend space-time, you can step to a distant location instantly. Or a distant time."

"And they're doing this at Montauk?" Michael asked.

Mr. Carradine gave a small, dry laugh. "Not anymore," he said. "They started to run into problems around 1988. The project was super secret, as you might imagine, but there were signs that the cover might be blown. This was during the Cold War—the Berlin Wall hadn't come down, and the Soviet Union was still intact. There was a dissident named Enrico Chekov who defected to America and showed the CIA Russian satellite photos of a strange phenomenon. Fortunately the Russians didn't know what it was, but our people did: it was a huge bubble in space-time centered on the Montauk site. Chekov sold his copies of the photographs to a reporter from the *New York Times*, and we had to steal them back."

We? Opal thought. *Had Mr. Carradine been personally involved? He was with the CIA, so he might well have been.* Aloud she said, "But the reporter saw them. Wouldn't he want to investigate further?"

"We shot him," Carradine said coolly. They stared at him, wondering if he was joking.

After a moment, Danny asked, "What about Chekov?"

"Him too," Carradine said. He straightened his jacket. "We kept the lid on that one, but it was a close call, and shortly afterward there was a major accident that killed seven of our best scientists and nearly eighty military personnel."

"What happened?" Danny asked.

"That information is on a need-to-know basis. You don't need to know."

Danny shrugged. "Fine."

"After the accident, Project Rainbow was closed down for the second time—this time by presidential order. It was one of the last things Ronald Reagan did before he left office. Except . . ." He pursed his lips. "And this is the part that goes beyond top secret, so please bear in mind it is not to be discussed with *anyone* outside this room, whatever their security clearance. The scientists found they couldn't close down the space-time distortion they'd created."

"I don't understand," Michael said.

Opal's father broke in again. "They created a rift in space-time using ultrahigh-powered magnetic fields. They assumed that when they shut the power down, the rift would disappear. But it didn't. Apparently when you tear space-time, it stays torn."

"You mean there's a time tunnel at Montauk?" Fuchsia asked. She looked delighted.

Mr. Carradine shrugged. "Actually *tunnel* gives the wrong idea. A tunnel goes in a straight line from one place to another. This is a rift in space-time. While we had the magnets on, we could control where it went. Now that they're off, it could lead anywhere."

"Or any*when*," Fuchsia added.

"Or anywhen," Carradine confirmed.

"What did they do about the presidential order?" Danny asked.

"They set up a very sophisticated alarm system that would trigger if the rift was activated. From the other side, so to speak. Very unlikely, of course, since you need high-tech equipment, but nobody wanted to take chances. Then they sealed the chamber under seven thousand tons of reinforced concrete."

"So Mr. Reagan left office happy." Danny grinned.

"I should think so," Carradine said. "I'm not sure anybody actually told him about the little difficulty."

Opal said, "Mr. Carradine, why are you sending us to Montauk?"

"Ah," said Carradine. He looked across at Sir Roland.

Sir Roland said flatly, "The idiots are opening up the rift chamber again."

"Well, I wouldn't necessarily call them idiots," Carradine said. "There's a great deal of scientific potential in that rift if we can solve the safety problems."

"Not to mention political potential," Sir Roland said, a little sourly. Opal knew her father very well, and it sounded to her as if there might be some differences of opinion with Mr. Carradine on this mission.

Carradine said easily, "Certainly if America can control the rift properly, it would virtually assure the security of the free world. It could become a conduit for cheap energy, for one thing. In the past, we used it mainly as a transporter—sending agents to various time periods. But if we modify the machinery, some scientists believe, it may be possible to pump heat direct from one of the prehistoric supervolcanoes. In any case, as Sir Roland says, our new president is interested in reviving the project. We started drilling down about a month ago. Now we're within striking distance of the chamber."

Opal said politely, "I'm sorry, Mr. Carradine, I still don't understand why you want to send a Shadow Project team to Montauk."

Carradine looked at her directly. "The alarm we installed went off two days ago."

Danny, Mid-Atlantic at 36,000 Feet

It was the first time Danny had been on a transatlantic aircraft, and he didn't like it. The plane was a 747 and half empty because of a terrorist scare, so it should have been comfortable, but it wasn't. Danny wasn't a particularly tall boy—in fact his Nan had once remarked how short his legs were—but there still wasn't enough room in his seat. He might have lost himself in the in-flight movie, except he'd seen it before, and it had been lousy first time round. The stale taste of recycled air gave him a headache.

But he could put up with discomfort—he hadn't exactly led a cushy life. What was getting to him was nerves. He didn't like the way the engine noise would suddenly vary as if there was something wrong. He didn't like the turbulence that sometimes got so bad it felt as if the plane would shake apart. He didn't like the way the redheaded flight attendant kept running up the center aisle with a worried look on her face. He didn't like the feeling there was a thin skin of aluminum underneath his seat, then nothing for 36,000 feet. Most of all, he didn't like the way the wing was moving.

Danny and the others had been booked onto a flight to New York. Each reservation was made separately as a routine security precaution, with seating spaced out so that they didn't appear to be traveling as a team. (Michael was lounging in first class now, having drawn the lucky straw.) Shortly after they boarded, Danny had helped himself to an empty window seat, after deciding he would be less nervous if he was able to look outside. Now he was looking out at the wing and feeling more nervous than ever.

Somebody slid into the empty seat beside him. "Doesn't it look amazing?" a voice asked. "Like a cotton-wool floor. I feel as if I could climb out there and dance across it like a fairy."

Danny glanced away from the threatening wing to find Fuchsia had joined him (against all orders!) and was staring past him through the window at the fluffy cloud layer fifty feet below. She was wearing an orange top with a floral miniskirt over thick, lime-green woolen tights. "Does that wing look all right to you?" he asked.

Fuchsia leaned across him and stared at the wing.

"It's not on fire," she said seriously.

"No, but it's moving up and down—see?"

"So it is! Just a little." Fuchsia smiled at him.

"You don't think it might snap off?"

"The wing? Oh, it can't," Fuchsia said brightly. "They don't attach two wings to a plane with glue or rivets or whatever. It's just one big wing that goes all the way through."

Danny looked at her, then looked back out. "It is?" he asked. "Is it really?"

"Really." Fuchsia nodded. "My uncle told me and he's a pilot."

"Oh, good." Danny glanced at the cotton-wool clouds. They did look as if you could get out and walk on them. "We're not supposed to sit together," he said, suddenly remembering.

"No, we're not—isn't it silly?" She gave him another of her smiles. "I'll go back in a minute. I just came over to find out if you have a girlfriend."

"Sorry?"

"A girlfriend. Are you going out with Opal or somebody?"

Not likely, Danny thought. "Opal's going out with Michael," he said. "I'm not going out with anybody."

Fuchsia's smile widened. "Just wanted to let you

know I'm available," she said. She patted his knee lightly, then tripped back to her seat.

Danny watched her go. After a moment he remembered to close his mouth.

[4]

Michael, Disused Air Force Base, Montauk, New York

Montauk was not what Michael had expected. The old air force base looked abandoned. A KEEP OUT warning sign was almost wholly overgrown with grass. The perimeter fence was broken down in several places. There were weeds poking through the concrete of the runways. His car stopped outside a gateway that was hanging from one hinge. Inside the fence, portions of the base looked like a construction site. He could hear the growl of earth-moving machinery and the clank of cranes. Workmen in hard hats lumbered about unloading materials. They seemed to be renovating one of the old buildings.

"You got your ID?" his driver asked him. Michael nodded. The driver was sharply dressed in a gray suit and wore shades straight out of Central Casting, but he still managed to look like a boxer. He had to be with one of the agencies, but he'd flatly refused to give out any information on the trip from the airport. Now he climbed out of the car and held open Michael's door like a chauffeur. "This is as far as I take you," he said. "Don't have clearance to go any farther. You must be mixed up in some heavy stuff."

"Where do I go?" Michael asked, ignoring the comment.

"Tell any of the workmen you're here to see Mr. Allen." The driver glanced through the gate and gave the ghost of a smile. "If you get that far."

He didn't. Although the base seemed deserted outside the construction area, he walked fewer than a dozen steps before a uniformed security officer emerged from one of the broken-down buildings. "Michael Potolo?" she said pleasantly. He noticed the uniform was of a private security firm, but all the same she was armed and, despite the pleasant tone, her hand rested casually on the butt of the pistol in her belt. Whatever the superficial appearances, somebody was taking security very seriously round here.

Michael nodded. "Yes, ma'am. Here to see Mr. Allen."

She smiled at him. "Mind if I check your ID?"

Michael handed her his Shadow Project papers and waited. She checked the photo ID carefully before handing them back. "Know what, Michael? You surely have a cute accent."

Michael smiled back. "Thank you. Is there really a Mr. Allen?"

She shook her head. "You're liaising with Colonel Saltzman. This operation is under military jurisdiction. You want to follow me, Michael? The others are already with him."

Colonel Saltzman was not what Michael expected either. He was a slender, balding man in his fifties, wearing a sour expression and a civilian suit that made him look like a constipated bank manager. His office had the appearance of something a bank manager would use as well—large computer desk, filing cabinet, and a scattering of chairs, but nothing else. Opal and the others, including Gary Carradine, were occupying those chairs now.

"Michael Potolo, sir," said Michael's escort. "That's everybody now."

"Thank you, Captain," Saltzman said.

"Captain?" Michael echoed in surprise. He glanced at his security guard.

"Captain Alison Woods," she said quietly. "Don't let the uniforms fool you—nothing's what it seems around here." She snapped off a quick salute to the colonel, then left. As the door closed behind her, Michael found himself thinking of a saying from his native Mali: *What you see, it's not what you think.*

Colonel Saltzman pinched the bridge of his nose in a

tired gesture and scowled. "Okay, we got a situation here, and they tell me you guys can help." He looked from one face to another, with the bewildered expression of someone examining the evidence from an alien autopsy. "You're psychics—right?"

No one seemed in a hurry to answer him before Mr. Carradine said, "Not exactly, Colonel."

The colonel stared at him for a moment. "You're an American, Mr. Carradine?"

"Yes, sir."

"CIA from what they tell me?"

Carradine nodded. "Currently with the Shadow Project in Britain, but yes: I'm still CIA."

"So tell me, Mr. Carradine, what's a CIA operative doing mixed up with a bunch of kids from *The Twilight Zone*?"

Mr. Carradine gave a slight smile, but Michael could tell he was not particularly amused. Even in the short time Michael had been with the Shadow Project, he'd realized Mr. Carradine felt protective toward his operatives.

Carradine said carefully, "Let me see if I understand the situation here, Colonel. The government has authorized a revival of the Montauk Project, and we've been drilling to open up the old space-time rift. That about the size of it?"

"Yes."

Carradine said softly, "I believe the alarm has gone off, Colonel Saltzman."

A wary look entered Saltzman's eyes. "Yes."

"Which means something from another place, another time—from outside of our reality, in fact—could be trying to get in." He stopped, holding the colonel's gaze and raising one eyebrow.

The colonel shifted uncomfortably. "I suppose you could put it that way."

"What other way would you like to put it?" Mr. Carradine asked. When the colonel was silent, Carradine said, "Let's cut the bull, Colonel. Somebody has convinced the president that the old Project Rainbow may have stumbled on an answer to the energy crisis, and an order has come down to reopen the space-time rift. If you stop drilling, the president is going to be very unhappy. But if you keep going, you have no idea what you might let through. We both know what happened in the old days. You're in trouble here, and my people—these *kids* as you call them—are the only ones who can bail you out. They're not psychics and they're not circus freaks. They're trained operatives with a very special talent—and that talent could be the solution to your problem."

There was a long, tense silence, then Saltzman's shoulders suddenly slumped. "I'm sorry, Mr. Carradine.

You're right. They dumped this whole thing in my lap when the alarm went off, and I've only had a few hours' sleep since then. Makes me tetchy." He looked around the group. "Okay, what's the plan?"

Fifteen minutes later they were gathered round a plan of the Montauk underground complex spread across the colonel's desk and weighted down by a variety of objects, including his cell phone and, alarmingly, his sidearm. The place, Michael thought, was huge—almost twice the size of the Shadow Project. That was pretty much the American way. They liked to do things bigger and better than the British.

"Of course, it's been abandoned for years," Colonel Saltzman remarked, as if reading his thoughts. "But I remember Jack Mullan telling me that when Project Rainbow was at its height, there were three thousand people down there—scientists, armed forces personnel, clerical, and catering staff. It was like a small town. Jack—Admiral Mullan—had the time of his life running it. Pity he's not here to see the project revived." He hesitated, then turned to Opal. "I don't know if it makes any difference to you, young lady, but your target is deep underground—the whole place was built to withstand a nuclear hit."

Like the Shadow Project, Michael thought.

Carradine said, "It won't make a difference." He

pointed to a section of the map. "This is our target—right?"

"That's right. The rift chamber itself is intact, but it's sealed four sides top and bottom with specially reinforced concrete. We're drilling through here." He pointed. "Approaching from the southwest."

"Is that all those big bulldozers and things we saw coming in?" Fuchsia asked.

The colonel shook his head. "No, that's part of our cover operation to mask any vibration or noise and give us an excuse to move in heavy machinery. We're supposed to be doing renovations on the base with a view to giving it back to the air force. But the real work is underground. We have an industrial auger down there, biggest SOB you've ever seen. We were just a few hours off the chamber when the alarm went off. We stopped drilling, of course."

"We'll go in from where you stopped," Carradine said decisively. "Opal doesn't like projecting through solid objects, so the shorter the distance she has to travel, the better. I assume you've still got an electrical feed into the sealed chamber?"

The colonel nodded. "Sure thing. Otherwise the alarm couldn't have gone off."

"We'll have to switch some lights on, or she won't be able to see. Apart from that . . ." Carradine trailed off vaguely. "I can't think of any other preparations."

"When can we do it?" Saltzman asked him.

"I'm expecting some equipment from Langley," Carradine said. "We can go when it arrives."

"There was a crate delivered for you a couple of hours ago," the colonel said. "Arrived just before you did."

Carradine glanced at Opal, who nodded slightly. "In that case, Colonel," Carradine said briskly, "if you can show me the way, we can go now."

Opal, Underground Base, Montauk

Tell me something, Mr. Carradine, if it's not classified information," Colonel Saltzman said. "Why four operatives?"

Carradine smiled slightly. "I guess your clearance is high enough for me to answer that, Colonel. We flew four operatives across because remote viewing is a two-person job. Opal here will do the viewing, but Michael's her partner and acts as her anchor—it stops psychological damage while she's out of the body. It's a technical thing. It has to do with the energies our equipment generates."

Opal liked the way Mr. Carradine had described Michael as her partner, even though it only meant they worked together on Project operations. Colonel Saltzman said, "What about the other two?"

"Backup," Mr. Carradine told him. "This is too important an op to leave anything to chance. Danny's as talented at the work as Opal, although he's not as experienced. And Fuchsia"—the smile widened slightly—"well, you mustn't judge a book by the way it dresses, Colonel."

They were walking together, all six of them, through the deserted corridors of the old Project Rainbow complex. Their footsteps echoed eerily and the whole place was in gloom, but the power was on and some minimal systems were still operative. Strip lights in the ceiling came on automatically as they walked, then switched off behind them, creating weird islands of illumination with darkness behind and darkness ahead. The effect was positively spooky, which was no help at all to Opal's nerves.

She tuned out the conversation between the colonel and Mr. Carradine and tried to concentrate on steadying herself. Her job, after all, was purely routine. She could actually have done it without leaving Britain, if they'd given her coordinates for the underground chamber, but Mr. Carradine had told her there were political implications to the mission. Those in charge of the revived Project Rainbow were extremely skeptical about remote viewing: it was hard enough to convince them it would work at all, let alone that it could work from thousands of miles away. "Why try to convince them?" Opal had asked. "We're the ones doing them a favor." Which was when Mr. Carradine explained that if she did a good job here, it could mean extra funding. This operation was so important, it could even outweigh her recent success in finding the terrorist leader Venskab Faivre aka the Skull. *So not much pressure there, then,* Opal thought. But however important the mission was, the fact remained it was a very simple job. All they wanted was for her to pass through less than a hundred yards of concrete—which she could manage almost instantaneously—then report back on what she found in the time-tunnel chamber. *Probably nothing,* Mr. Carradine had said. *Probably just a fault in the alarm system.* But what if there *was* something . . . ?

The trouble was, she kept wondering what the *something* might be. Nobody had told her much about the rift: typical need-to-know mentality. So she was left to imagine the sort of thing that might trigger an alarm. Maybe some kind of animal from the distant past that had wandered into the time rift. Once you established a rift like that, it might lead *anywhere.* There was even the possibility that what had triggered the alarm was a visitor from the future, and heaven alone knew what that might be—a highly evolved human with a massive brain who could control people with a single thought, or maybe some alien creature from outer space that had taken over the planet in a million years' time.

There had definitely been trouble in the past, but

nobody would say what. She'd talked about it with her father just before she left. He'd told her confidentially he thought the scientists had been mad to open the rift in the first place and doubly mad to unseal it again now. They clearly didn't know enough to manage it safely.

Colonel Saltzman stopped by a door, sturdily made from new wood. He fished a key from his pocket and unlocked it. "In here," he murmured, and led them through. The doorway itself was so small he had to stoop a little, but when Opal followed him she found herself in a large concrete tunnel that looked for all the world like a gigantic sewer pipe. The lighting here was strictly temporary—bulbs strung along electric cord—but at least it was consistent so that the whole tunnel was lit. This was obviously the passage the army had been drilling toward the rift chamber. "Take it slow," the colonel advised. "We haven't gotten around to flattening a floor yet."

Maybe it was worse if you had big feet like the colonel, because Opal didn't really find it tricky at all; besides, they had only to walk a few hundred yards before the tunnel came to an end, the way blocked by a drilling machine so gigantic that it seemed like something from a science fiction movie. Beside it, a team of men in white coats were unpacking and assembling electronic equipment from a wooden crate. Something about the gear looked vaguely familiar, but Opal still hadn't decided what it was before Mr. Carradine said sharply, "I didn't know your men were familiar with psychotronic machinery, Colonel."

"Those aren't my men, Mr. Carradine," the colonel told him easily. "They're yours. Turned up an hour after the crate, flashing their CIA IDs and throwing their weight around. Thought they'd be out of the way down here, and they seemed happy enough."

"Didn't recognize them," Carradine said sheepishly. "Excuse me, Colonel." He walked over to the technicians and started a quiet conversation.

Colonel Saltzman glanced toward Opal. "Suppose you know all about this gear, young lady?"

Opal realized that in fact she did. What was taking shape out of the crate looked like a portable version of the Shadow Project's own projection equipment, the psychotronic helmets that helped agents out of their physical bodies and dispatched them to specific, distant coordinates. She also realized she quite liked the colonel, with his laid-back attitude and his Southern drawl. "I think it may be something to help me do my job." She smiled.

Fifteen minutes later, she and Michael were seated side by side, wearing skeletal versions of the familiar Shadow Project headgear. The CIA technicians had been banished, and Mr. Carradine was making final adjustments on a laptop computer. "Interesting that they have this equipment at Langley," Michael said quietly.

"What's Langley?" Opal asked him.

"CIA headquarters in Virginia. Some of the gear we're using here is more advanced than the psychotronics we have back in Britain, but the CIA has always claimed their remote viewing project has been closed down for years."

"You don't think the CIA would *lie* to us?" Opal asked him, poker-faced.

Carradine glanced up from his laptop. "The coordinates are set. You two ready?"

"Are you ready, Michael?" Opal asked.

"You're the one who's traveling," Michael told her. "I'll just sit here and wait for you to come back safely."

"We're ready, Mr. Carradine," Opal called. She took a deep breath to try to settle herself.

She expected Mr. Carradine to trigger the equipment, but instead he said, frowning, "One thing, Opal, and this is important." He stared at her for emphasis, then went on, "Your job is to examine the chamber that houses the time tunnel, look around for anything that might have set off the alarm. But under no circumstances are you to enter the rift itself. That is positively, absolutely forbidden. Okay?"

Opal had not the slightest intention of going near

the time rift. "Perfectly clear, Mr. Carradine," she said. Actually, the time tunnel was the last thing she was thinking about. She still couldn't shake the feeling there might be something scary lurking in the chamber, maybe even something that had evolved enough to sense her energy body.

"We've no idea what effect a space-time distortion might have on your second body," Carradine said. "It might even destroy it, so keep well clear."

"I will," Opal promised.

"Did he say 'second body'?" Colonel Saltzman murmured, half to himself.

"We're ready, Mr. Carradine," Opal said again.

Carradine reached for his laptop.

Fuchsia jerked as if she'd just been stung. "Something's wrong!"

But it was too late. Mr. Carradine had pressed the ENTER key.

[6]

Opal, Out-of-Body, Underground

Something was wrong. It was different from the way things happened in the Shadow Project. There you had a brief flash of scenery, then you were at your destination, feeling perfectly normal, perfectly solid, but actually occupying a second body that could walk through walls like a ghost. So she should be in the time-tunnel chamber now, but she wasn't. She was floating in darkness. She could no longer tell which way was up. Any attempt at movement led to more confusion. A wave of nausea swept over her.

Opal forced herself to stay calm. The most likely explanation was that Mr. Carradine had been given the wrong coordinates. It sometimes happened on missions. Usually the error was small, so you arrived only a few yards from your expected destination and it didn't matter . . . if you even noticed at all. But a shortfall in her present mission would leave her inside the concrete plug in total darkness—exactly where she seemed to be now. It made sense; and all she had to do was figure out the direction of the time-tunnel chamber and move toward it. In moments she would emerge from the plug and complete her mission.

Unless, a worried voice whispered in her mind, the wrong coordinates had placed her in the time tunnel itself.

Despite all attempts at discipline, Opal felt a creeping panic. Mr. Carradine had warned her to stay well clear of the tunnel, and she knew exactly why. No one really understood the physics of space-time. For all she knew, the rift could send her consciousness anywhere, to any time or place. Alternatively, it might rip her energy body to shreds, compress it, expand it, or drive her insane like those poor sailors in the Philadelphia Experiment. It could—

With an almost superhuman effort, Opal pushed the panic aside. She still felt afraid—very much afraid—but she forced herself to think clearly. First of all, her second body *hadn't* been ripped to shreds, nor harmed in any way so far as she could tell. And she wasn't any more of a lunatic than usual. She was simply somewhere in darkness, a little confused, and the most likely explanation for that was *definitely* a shortfall in the coordinates, leaving her inside the concrete plug. And since she didn't know which way to go to reach the rift chamber, it would make sense to return to her physical body and try again.

Gross movement follows thought. It was the first thing operatives were taught when they joined the Shadow Project. If you needed to go somewhere in your second body, you visualized your destination clearly and it drew you to the target like a magnet. If she was inside the concrete plug, her physical body was only yards away at most. It should be the easiest thing in the world to return to it and start again. She took a deep breath and turned her attention to the scene she'd just left: herself in the chair; Michael seated beside her; Mr. Carradine fiddling with his laptop; Danny, Fuchsia, and the colonel looking on. . . .

Nothing happened.

Opal closed her eyes and visualized as vividly as she could, this time concentrating only on her physical body seated on its chair. During Shadow Project training, they referred to your physical body as the *prime objective*. It was your ultimate anchor, the one thing you could rely on when all else failed. But still nothing happened. Maybe the problem had something to do with the closeness of the space-time rift. She wondered if she could contact Michael. They were linked, brain waves to brain waves, through the electronics of the psychotronic helmets, and sometimes, under rare circumstances, the linkage could be made almost telepathic so that he could experience flashes of her thoughts and she of his. She tried desperately to send him a mental message, but if Michael heard her, he didn't manage to reply. She was alone in the darkness.

But that was all right, Opal thought, still fighting back the panic: she could swim out if she kept her head. Swimming was a technique they taught all agents of the Shadow Project as an emergency approach to situations just like this, where it was extraordinarily difficult to judge direction, how fast you were moving, or, indeed, whether you were actually moving at all. For some reason, the actions of swimming gave you back an accurate sensation of movement. You were even able to judge approximately how fast you were traveling. Which only left the question of direction.

Opal tried to work things out logically. Although confused and disoriented, she had not turned around since she found herself in the darkness. Or at least she didn't think she'd turned around. Which meant that any shortfall would still have left her facing the target chamber. So if she swam in that direction, she should emerge from the encasing concrete quite quickly. And even if she had turned without noticing it, there was a two-to-one chance that swimming would still bring her into the light. If she'd turned around, she would swim back toward Michael and the others. If she'd turned upward, she would emerge on the surface. Only if she found herself swimming downward would she be in really serious trouble.

Opal launched herself forward and swam. But as the seconds stretched to minutes, velvet darkness still embraced her.

[7]

Danny, Underground at Montauk

Carradine's head jerked round. "What's the matter?"

Danny started forward. Fuchsia was in trouble. Her pale face had taken on a bluish tinge so that it was positively corpselike. Her hands were clenched tightly, and she seemed to be having problems breathing. He took her arm. "Are you all right?"

Fuchsia's eyes rolled back and upward, so she looked like something in a horror movie. There was a catch in her throat as she rasped, "It's bad. Very bad."

"What's bad?" Danny asked, frightened. Was she choking? Her knees buckled suddenly, and he threw his arms around her to stop her from falling. She was dead-weight, surprisingly heavy for such a slight, slim girl. Then Carradine was beside them.

"Let her down on the floor," Carradine said. "It's all right."

"It's not all right," Danny said. "She's fainted or something."

"It's what she does," Carradine said, bewilderingly. "Just let her down to the floor. Gently."

Danny glanced at Carradine, then did as he was told. Fuchsia's head rolled to one side as he laid her down. Her eyes were closed now and she was no longer choking, although she was taking long, slow, rattling breaths. Carradine knelt beside her. "Blackness," she murmured. "Blackness and death."

"Did she say 'death'?" Danny asked. What the hell was going on here?

"The kid's sick?" asked Colonel Saltzman. "You want me to send for a medic?"

"She's fine," Carradine insisted. "It's what she does," he said again.

"She's not fine!" Danny snapped. Any fool could see she wasn't fine. Maybe she was having a seizure or something. Except she wasn't twitching: just lying there and breathing like a rusty engine. He knelt beside Carradine. "Let the colonel get a doctor."

"Trust me," Carradine hissed. To Fuchsia he said quietly, "Is Opal all right?"

"How would she know?" Danny asked belligerently. "Can't you see she's not well?"

"Darkness." Fuchsia moaned as if she were in pain.

"Opal's in the dark?" Carradine asked. "Will she tell you this?"

"She said 'death' a minute ago," Danny muttered.

Carradine was all right, at least not the worst of them, but Danny didn't like what he was doing now. He didn't seem to care if Fuchsia was sick. And what did he mean, *Will Opal tell you this?*

"Yes," Fuchsia said. It came out on a long, shuddering breath.

From the chair behind them, Opal stirred. Danny glanced around quickly. Her eyes were open, but blank and staring. Seated beside her, their helmets linked by a single cable, Michael looked asleep, but his face was tranquil.

Carradine said, "Can you tell me anything else, Fuchsia?"

"What's going on here, Mr. Carradine?" Danny asked.

"You sure you don't want a medic?" This from the colonel, who was looking concerned.

Fuchsia's eyes slid shut.

"She's fainted!" Danny said accusingly.

The colonel said brusquely, "Mr. Carradine, you can do what you like, but I'm getting medical help. The kid's not well." He turned on his heel and walked off down the tunnel. Danny wondered why he didn't use his cell phone, then remembered they were deep underground, well out of range of any signal. He turned back to Fuchsia in time to see her open her eyes and sit up suddenly. She had the dazed look of somebody waking from a particularly deep sleep, but as she focused on him, she gave a slow, dazzling smile. "Hello, Danny."

"Are you all right?" Danny asked.

"Oh, yes," Fuchsia said. "It's really sweet of you to ask."

"Can you remember any of that?" Carradine asked her.

Fuchsia shook her head. "I'm sorry, Mr. Carradine. Not this time." She frowned. "But I knew something had gone wrong before I went under."

"Yes, you told us. When you went under, you said something about darkness." Carradine looked at her expectantly.

"I'm sorry." Fuchsia shrugged helplessly.

"What's going on here, Mr. Carradine?" Danny asked.

Carradine glanced after the retreating form of the colonel and obviously decided he was out of earshot. "You're going to find out eventually, Danny. Fuchsia has a special talent."

Danny looked at him blankly. "Like, out-of-body? The rest of us can do that."

Carradine shook his head. "We're still testing Fuchsia for out-of-body abilities, but early on something else came up. She seems to be a functioning precog."

"She can see the *future*?" Danny exclaimed. He didn't think that sort of stuff existed outside of Marvel Comics.

Fuchsia said coyly, "Oh that makes it sound like such a big deal, Danny. I don't have much control over it, but Mr. Carradine says the Project might be able to fix that eventually." She smiled at him again. "Until they do, it's usually just . . . you know . . . flashes like I had about you and me."

Like I had about you and me? Danny was opening his mouth to ask her what all *that* meant when Opal said, "I'm back."

[8]

Michael, Underground at Montauk

Michael's eyes snapped open and he looked around. His mind was fuzzy from the anchor dream—as often happened, he'd found himself back with the Dogon in his native Mali—but he still realized there was something wrong. Danny and Mr. Carradine were kneeling beside Fuchsia, who was sitting on the floor for some reason. Michael turned his head quickly to see if Opal was all right and found her calmly unfastening her helmet. She gave him a little smile.

"Tu vas bien?" he asked her quietly, then realized he'd reverted to his native French and translated, "You okay?"

Opal set the helmet down and combed her hair with her fingers. "I'm fine. Little bit of trouble with the projection, but I worked it out eventually." She glanced across at the others. "What's happened?"

"I don't know," Michael said. He started to remove his helmet.

Mr. Carradine was climbing to his feet. He offered

a hand to Fuchsia, who took it and stood up too, a little unsteadily. Carradine called over his shoulder to Opal, "Any problems?"

"I was in the dark for a time," Opal said. "I undershot the target—I think the coordinates the colonel gave us must have been a little off."

"No, it was an equipment problem," Fuchsia said.

Danny, who was on his feet now too, glanced at her quickly. "How do you know?"

"The battery pack is underpowered," Fuchsia murmured, as if that explained how she knew.

Carradine asked Opal, "What happened?"

Opal shrugged. "I got confused. I came out-of-body and into the concrete they used to seal off the chamber rather than the time-tunnel chamber itself. There's no point of reference when that happens, so I wasn't sure of the direction."

"Did you swim?"

She nodded. "I managed to go downward, unfortunately." She gave a small smile. "But I realized I was wrong before I reached the center of the Earth. So I reversed direction and eventually came up in one of the offices. Once I was oriented, I was able to refocus on Michael and the rest of you."

"So you just came back to your body?" Carradine sounded disappointed.

But Opal shook her head. "No. I came back here all right, but then I tried a direct line to the target chamber straight through the plug. Which worked." She looked smug.

"Well done!" Carradine exclaimed. He glanced around. "Can't debrief you without the colonel. What the hell's keeping him?"

"Where's he gone?" Opal frowned.

Danny said, "Went to get a doctor. He thought Fuchsia was sick. She's an operational precog."

Michael frowned. "What's an operational precog?"

"Somebody who can see into the future, according to Mr. Carradine," Danny told him. They all turned in Carradine's direction.

Carradine laughed. "All right, all right, I'll fill you in. What—" He stopped. Running footsteps were sounding in the tunnel, and in a moment Colonel Saltzman appeared, accompanied by a young officer in Medical Corps uniform. "Later," Carradine finished hurriedly.

The young officer zeroed in on Fuchsia after a nod from his colonel. "Colonel says you're feeling poorly, miss?"

"I'm fine," Fuchsia insisted. "Are you going to take my blood pressure?"

In fact, the doctor did take her blood pressure, examine her eyes, and sound her chest with a stethoscope.

"She seems okay now," he said to the colonel.

"Told you," Fuchsia said.

They waited until the doctor left, then Carradine said, "Opal made it to the target chamber, Colonel."

"You really can tell me what's in there? What set the alarm off?" He still sounded doubtful.

Opal shrugged slightly. "Nothing, so far as I can see."

They looked at her blankly.

"The rift—the time tunnel or whatever you want to call it—is still there. I could see it quite plainly." She shuddered involuntarily. "It's very peculiar to look at when you're in your second body."

"And while you're in your first one," Carradine murmured. Michael glanced across at him. He kept wondering if Mr. Carradine had been associated with the original Project Rainbow.

"The good news," Opal said, "is that there's nothing nasty in there. I looked very carefully—there's really nowhere to hide."

"So what set off the alarm, little lady?" the colonel asked. "Or was it just a glitch in the system?"

"I think it must have been," Opal told him. "Maybe it was the vibration of the drill. But anyway, there's nothing in the chamber that shouldn't be there."

"So it's safe for us to open it up again?"

Opal said carefully, "I can't give you guarantees, but

I could see no problem."

The colonel gave a relieved smile. "Okay, that'll have to be good enough for me." He turned away from her. "Mr. Carradine, looks like we're going in."

Michael, the Montauk Carlton, Montauk

The breakfast room was empty of guests when Michael came down, and empty of staff too as far as he could see, but there was a table set for five with Mr. Carradine's name tag leaning on a tiny jar of marmalade, so he took one of the places and waited patiently. There were bowls of cereal and fruit set out on a table to one side, but he thought it best to wait. Mr. Carradine had booked them all into one of the more anonymous hotels in Montauk, and the others should be down soon.

His thumb made a circling movement of its own accord.

Michael watched it happen and felt a sudden chill. The silence in the breakfast room grew louder, and beyond it he could hear intrusive traffic noises from the street outside. He could hear his own breathing. He could hear the steady pulse of blood within his veins. He became aware of the smell of raw sausages, drifting from the refrigerator in some distant kitchen. He could smell tomatoes and the musty scent of mushrooms and bacon and milk in an open carton and a farmyard hint of eggs.

He needed to get back to his room.

Time slowed as Michael began to push his chair away from the table—it made a hideous scraping noise on the wooden floor—so that he watched the waitress bustle over in a series of strobelike jumps. "Hi, honey," she said cheerfully, her voice reverberating through his head. "Sorry to keep you waiting." She handed him a laminated menu, and his nerveless fingers dropped it on the table with the sound of a felled tree.

"Have to get something from my room," Michael muttered. He tried to push past her.

She gave him a big smile. "Your friends are on their way down," she told him.

In fact his friends were in the corridor outside. He could smell Mr. Carradine's aftershave. He could hear a conversation about jazz between Opal and Danny. They were coming through the door in a tight little group with Mr. Carradine in the lead. Time was distorting like mad now, and when he looked at Opal he could hear her heartbeat. It grew faster when she saw him. Michael pushed the waitress rudely aside and strode across the room. The floor felt spongy underneath his feet.

"Michael," Opal called out brightly, "we're not going

home today. Mr. Carradine has arranged for us to stay on so we can watch the chamber being opened." She sounded pleased.

Michael said, "Getting something from my room." He tried to smile.

Mr. Carradine said, "Are you okay, Michael?"

"Fine," Michael told him. It came out something close to a gasp. He kept moving with a purposeful stride, and to his relief they parted to let him through.

"Have you had breakfast?" Opal called after him, but he ignored her.

He thought there might be a problem with the stairs, but he almost floated up them. By the time he reached the corridor that led to his room, he was running, with the walls pulsating in time to each step. He reached his door and fumbled for the key card. The room next door was empty, but he could hear what was going on in a room along the corridor: a bitter argument between a husband and wife over some item of jewelry she'd bought. From another room he could hear snoring. In another he could smell the lavatory cleaner as a maid prepared a bathroom. His hand was shaking so badly he couldn't insert the card. He closed his eyes to a maelstrom of whirling colors, opened them, and tried again.

The card slid into the slot. He pulled it out, carefully, and listened to an electronic symphony as the little red light turned to green. He pressed the handle and pushed the door.

His consciousness expanded to take in part of the town. There was a heavy-metal beat coming from a building down the road.

Michael's eyes rolled back as he slid to the floor, then closed as he reached it. His body began to twitch, then shake, then convulse violently. A moan escaped his lips, but Michael did not hear it. His head began to pound against the carpet with dull, sickly thuds, in perfect time to the rock music playing in the distant building.

[10]

Fuchsia, Underground at Montauk

It was almost impossible to hear above the noise of the auger, which screeched, rattled, shook, and boomed like constant thunder, so Fuchsia ignored the shouted conversations and entertained herself by surreptitiously watching Danny. He wasn't a conventionally handsome boy—Michael was far better-looking—but he had nice eyes and a cheeky grin. Fuchsia sneezed. There was a lot of dust in the tunnel and it tickled her sinuses. She pulled a little handkerchief from her sleeve, dabbed her nose, and looked around.

Despite Opal's all-clear, the nice colonel had brought in a small contingent of troops wearing battle gear and ear protectors, who were standing at ease just behind the head of the auger. The colonel himself was up in the cabin of the machine, beside the operator. Both were wearing hard hats and earmuffs. Danny was standing with Mr. Carradine well to the rear, where the sound was at a lower level. Opal and Michael were beside them, holding hands, which was sweet, although Michael looked a little off-color, Fuchsia thought, or maybe just tired or worried or something. Perhaps they'd had a fight and made up. Danny happened to glance in Fuchsia's direction, and she gave him a smile and a little wave.

The machine operator pulled a lever, and all the noise and vibration suddenly stopped, leaving Fuchsia with a ringing in her ears. The colonel climbed out of the cabin and dropped to the ground. He walked to his men and said something Fuchsia couldn't hear, which caused them to fan out in a semicircle, rifles at the ready. Mr. Carradine moved to join him, leaving the others where they were. Fuchsia took a casual step or two forward, so she was standing beside Danny. "What do you think is happening?" she asked him.

"Might be close to a breakthrough," Danny told her.

Mr. Carradine rejoined them. "I need you up front, Opal," he announced. "They're about to make the final thrust. The rest of you want to come too?"

"Just try to stop us," Michael said.

"You'll want these," Mr. Carradine said, handing out military-style ear protectors. "Bad enough up here, but it gets *really* noisy down there. Put them on before the auger starts up again. Opal, I want you to confirm the chamber is still exactly as you saw it—probably will be, but no sense in taking chances. The rest of you"—he smiled—"you're just along for the ride. Stand clear of the soldiers and try not to get in anybody's way."

The earmuffs reduced the sound level, but even so, the noise was so extreme that Fuchsia knew she'd have to move away again if it went on much longer. But then there was a massive cracking sound and the colonel, now on the ground, was signaling to the auger driver. The great machine reversed and rumbled slowly backward. It moved a long way up the tunnel, then cut its engine again. Fuchsia stared.

The auger had broken through one complete wall of the buried chamber. Despite the damage, the electricity supply still functioned and there were strip lights glowing from the ceiling inside. The chamber contained banks of computerized machinery, much of it very old-fashioned in design. Thick cables snaked toward two enormous upright metal slabs, each close on six feet thick, that ran from floor to ceiling. Between them—

Fuchsia suddenly felt sick. Between them was something that should not have existed, a roiling, pulsing *nothingness*, blacker than black, deeper than the universe and utterly, completely alien. She was looking at the rift in space-time, torn open by the metal slabs that had to be Project Rainbow's giant magnets. Her sole reaction was naked fear. She could not for an instant imagine how anyone would voluntarily enter that hideous space between the slabs. Yet she was certain Rainbow operatives must have done so in the course of their experiments . . . and probably would again, now that the chamber was reopened. It was a terrifying thought.

"Wow!" exclaimed a voice beside her. Danny.

Fuchsia fought down the urge to vomit and, with a massive effort, dragged her gaze away from the rift. She found she was shaking and took deep yoga breaths to steady herself. Beside her, Danny, Opal, Michael, the colonel, and Mr. Carradine were all staring, entranced, at the rift.

"So this is it, Mr. Carradine," the colonel said.

Carradine nodded.

"I'm supposed to check that the machinery is still working."

"Then you'd better do so, Colonel," Carradine said.

The colonel sniffed. "Thought you might like to do that for me, seeing as . . ." He let the sentence trail.

Carradine shrugged. "Okay." He walked over to the banks of equipment that flanked the rift itself and began to throw a sequence of switches. A humming sound filled the chamber, and a series of dials lit up.

He's done this before, Fuchsia thought.

"Seems to be running normally," Carradine murmured.

Fuchsia caught a slight movement out of the corner of her eye. She turned to find the rift had changed texture and was glowing slightly. On the floor between the magnetic pillars was a small plastic box that she was certain hadn't been there before.

The colonel must have spotted it as well, for he muttered, "Where the heck did that come from?" and strode across to pick it up.

"The Cobra!" Carradine whispered, so softly that only Fuchsia could have heard him. "Colonel—" he called anxiously.

The colonel picked up the box.

"—don't open—"

But the colonel was already flicking back the lid. He peered inside and frowned. "Glass vials with some sort of liquid. Three of them are broken." He reached in and took out a vial for inspection. "Looks like a urine sample." He glanced across at Carradine. "Did they have some sort of lab down here?"

Carradine said quietly, "Put it back, Colonel, and close the box. Now."

The colonel stared at him in surprise for a moment, then said, "Right." He put the vial back and clicked the lid shut. "Best get this to the science boys up top."

For some reason Fuchsia found herself thinking about the Greek myth of Pandora, who opened a box and released all the evils of the world.

[11]

Opal, the Montauk Carlton, Montauk

Opal awoke with a start.

For a long moment she couldn't work out where she was. The room was gloomy, but far from dark—a neon sign outside one window managed to throw a wash of color across the walls despite the curtains. Beyond the foot of her bed, she could see the outline of a television set looming over its own red standby light. Then she remembered: she was in the Montauk Carlton. She turned her head to confirm this and gasped in sudden panic. The space between her bed and the door was filled with alien white figures. Opal opened her mouth to scream.

"Miss Harrington," said the closest figure, and the only thing that stopped Opal from actually screaming was the fact that it was a woman's voice. "Miss Harrington, are you awake?"

Opal sat bolt upright, holding the bedclothes to her

throat. She was wearing only a short silk nightgown and felt extremely vulnerable. "Who are you? What do you want?" A hint of antiseptic wafted into her nostrils.

"Miss Harrington, you need to come with us. You have to get dressed at once."

"Who are you?" Opal repeated. She reached out and switched on her bedside lamp.

The woman was wearing a white suit of plastic material and some sort of headpiece that covered the whole of her face. Her eyes bored into Opal through transparent goggles. Three other suited figures—men to judge by their size—stood between her and the door. "We're from the Project," the woman said urgently. "Please, Miss Harrington, you must come with us at once. Have you had close contact with anyone since you left Colonel Saltzman? Anyone in the hotel?"

Frowning, Opal shook her head. "No, I came straight up to my room. What's going on?"

"We can discuss that on the way. We've alerted your father. Now can—"

"My father? What's my father got to do with it?"

But the woman and her companions were already pushing out of the room. "We'll give you privacy to get dressed," she said, "and talk on the way."

Opal stared for a moment at the closed door, then got up and headed for the wardrobe. A feeling of dread had settled in her stomach.

As she stepped from the room, they surrounded her and escorted her to the elevator, where another white-suited figure was holding the door. Opal had only the barest impression of the hotel lobby as she was ushered through to startled glances from staff and guests. There was an ambulance on the street outside. Opal stopped dead. "What's this? I'm not sick." But strong hands gripped her arms and she was frog-marched into the waiting vehicle. The woman and two of her companions climbed in with her.

As the ambulance pulled away, Opal looked from one silent figure to another and fought to keep calm. Eventually she said in her coldest voice, "This has gone far enough. If you want me to cooperate, you will have to tell me what is going on. Otherwise"—she fished her cell phone from her pocket and flicked it open—"I shall place a call to Colonel Saltzman and demand—"

"Colonel Saltzman is dead," said the woman beside her.

"What?"

"I'm sorry. I don't know any easy way to tell you this. The colonel is dead. Project Rainbow is now under the command of Brigadier General Tudor."

Opal stared at her, but the headgear made it impossible to read any expression. "Colonel Saltzman can't be dead. I was speaking to him only hours ago."

"Miss Harrington, I'm Dr. Amory—that's Major Helen Amory, Army Medical Corps, on assignment to Project Rainbow for the duration of the current emergency. Colonel—"

"What current emergency?" Opal interrupted.

"Miss Harrington, you and I will get on far better if you give me a chance to explain. Everyone here is cleared to hear what I have to say, and that may not be the case when we arrive, so I'd suggest you shut up and listen—okay?"

Opal shut up and listened.

"Miss Harrington," said Helen Amory, "I don't have the security clearance to know what Colonel Saltzman and his people were doing at Project Rainbow, but I've been told you and your friends were flown over from England to help. I also understand the CIA is involved here, as well as the army, maybe other agencies. Now, what I can tell you is this. Colonel Saltzman died just over an hour ago from a highly infectious disease. The disease is bacterial in origin, but resistant to our most powerful antibiotics. We tried seventeen of them on him, singly and in combination, and nothing touched his fever. We were still searching for an effective treatment when he died."

"He looked completely healthy when I saw him," Opal said, wide-eyed.

"It's one of the most virulent illnesses I have ever seen.

It's also one of the most infectious. Two of the nurses who looked after Colonel Saltzman are now fighting for their lives. One of his military personnel—Captain Alison Woods—was with him when he collapsed. She is now showing early symptoms."

"I met Captain Woods," Opal said. "She was in charge of security."

Dr. Amory glanced out the ambulance window, then turned back to Opal. "We've set up quarantine units in the old underground base. It's only a matter of time before we find an antibiotic that works, of course, but in the meantime we must isolate everyone who's been in contact with the disease."

"That's where you're taking me?" Opal said, half a question, half a statement.

Helen Amory nodded. "Yes."

"I don't feel ill," Opal told her.

"And hopefully you'll stay that way. But it's vital we keep this from spreading, and you and your friends were in contact with the colonel."

"So you're bringing in the others as well?"

Dr. Amory nodded again. "Yes."

"Will I be given treatment?" Opal asked.

"Not unless you get ill. We've only managed to set up a few treatment units so far, and they're all in use. The rest of the units are more like hospital wards, I'm afraid. Some of them were jail cells, dating from the time when Rainbow was first established. But we'll make you as comfortable as possible and you'll be fed army food, which isn't nearly as bad as you'd imagine."

"How long will you keep me isolated?"

"No more than a week," Helen Amory told her. "Unless you show symptoms."

"A *week*?" Opal exploded. "I'm supposed to fly home tomorrow—later today."

"If you're still symptom-free in forty-eight hours, it's unlikely you've been infected, but we need to be sure. A week to be on the safe side."

The woman was wearing an isolation suit, Opal realized abruptly. The very air she was breathing was filtered to remove bacteria. Opal had seen something similar in a movie about germ warfare. "And if I do start to show symptoms . . . ?"

Dr. Amory hesitated. "Hopefully we'll have found a cure by then."

After a moment, Opal said, "Do you know what you're dealing with yet? Some sort of superbug?"

"In a manner of speaking," Helen Amory said drily. "We're fairly certain Colonel Saltzman died of the Black Death."

[12]

Danny, in Quarantine, Underground at Montauk

Quarantine wasn't as bad as Danny had expected. It was certainly a lot better than the nights he'd spent in the slammer during his bad-boy days. He had a private room, for one thing: comfy bed, little desk thing with a phone on it, chairs, flat-screen TV screwed into the wall. Nobody locked the door, for another. Thing was, the whole team was in quarantine, but isolation units were limited and they weren't in quarantine from each other. No point really. They'd already been in close contact. If one had it, they all had it. So you could wander down the corridor and visit your friends if you liked, just so you didn't try to leave the isolation unit. Leaving the isolation unit was something else. Wasn't just a lockdown either: there were *armed guards* on every exit. Yanks weren't shy when it came to lethal force. You had to admire them.

He was lying on the comfy bed using the remote to

channel surf when Michael slipped furtively through the door.

"Knock?" Danny said.

"Sorry," Michael said, but gave no sign of going out again. He looked around for the nearest chair and sat in it. That's what irritated Danny about Michael: too self-confident by half. "Can I talk to you?" Michael asked. When there was no immediate reaction, he added, "About . . . something?"

Danny stared at him for a moment, then switched off the television and swung his feet off the bed onto the floor. About *something*? "Okay," he said cautiously.

"I'd like your advice," Michael said in his polite Eton accent.

"What about?" In the great scheme of things, *something* didn't convey a lot of information. Danny felt wary and vaguely suspicious. People didn't usually ask his advice. Especially African princes.

Michael looked uncomfortable. "You know when you join the Project, they give you a physical?" He hesitated, then added, as if Danny mightn't know what a physical was, "A medical examination?"

Danny nodded. "Yeah." The doctor who'd done his was cross-eyed with a hacking cough, a poor advertisement for his profession.

"Is it to make sure you're fit for the job, or do you

think it's just, you know, an insurance thing?"

This was getting weird, Danny thought. "Bit of both, I expect. How should I know?" This had to be something to do with the plague, but when Michael decided to pussyfoot around a subject, he was a real expert. All the same, Michael was looking genuinely worried.

"Did you tell them the truth?" Michael asked. "About your health?"

Not just weird but downright bewildering. "No reason not to—I'm healthy as a horse. Tonsils as a kid, but that's about it."

"Did you tell the doctor about your tonsils?"

"Can't remember," Danny said honestly. "But if I did, it didn't seem to worry him."

"Suppose it had been something more serious. Like . . . diabetes or"—he licked his lips nervously—"something else. Do you think they'd still have taken you on?"

"You don't have diabetes, do you?" Danny asked.

"No, no," said Michael quickly. "That was just an example. What I meant was, if you *had* a serious condition, would they still keep you on?"

"Do *you* have a serious condition?" Danny pushed him. If he did, Danny couldn't think what. Never so much as heard him sneeze. He'd seen Michael in the shower, and he was one of the fittest-looking blokes he knew.

Michael flushed, then shook his head. "No, of course not. I was just wondering. You know . . . about Project policy."

"You've been with the Project a year longer than I have," Danny told him. "You have to know more about policy than I do." What was *wrong* with Michael? There had to be something, or he'd never have started this conversation. Maybe he was worried about getting sick and it had affected his brain. Danny opened his mouth to say something else, then shut it again as Fuchsia came in, waving a book.

"Boys," Fuchsia said. "I've found what they're all so worried about."

"I'd better go," Michael muttered. He started to rise from his seat.

"No, you stay," Fuchsia told him. "I wanted to tell Danny, but we all need to know this."

Michael sat down again, warily. He gave a warning glance toward Danny, as if asking him not to mention what they'd been discussing, not that Danny knew what they had been discussing in the first place.

Fuchsia said, "It's the Black Death."

"What's the Black Death?"

"What they're all worrying we might have. Opal told me. But the thing is, I've looked it up now." She waved the book she was holding. "It was the most awful disease that broke out in the Middle Ages. Listen to this." She flicked the book open and read, "'The plague that raged all over the land consumed nine parts in ten of the men through England, scarcely leaving a tenth man alive.' That was from the records of the Bristol and Gloucestershire Archaeological Society in 1883."

"It broke out in 1883?" Danny asked.

"No, silly," Fuchsia said. "They're an *archaeological* society. They were reporting on old findings. But imagine nine people in ten wiped out! That's worse than those awful African diseases like Ebola that everybody's frightened of." She waved the book at them again. "It broke out in China in thirteen-something and spread to Europe a couple of years later. They called it the *blue sickness* then. People used to catch it in the morning, and by the afternoon they were *dead*. It was totally the fastest disease *ever*."

"Yes, but that was before antibiotics," Danny said. "They can cure it now, can't they?"

"That's the thing," Fuchsia told him. "They used to think it was bubonic plague, which is pretty nasty and fast and deadly, but this book says scientists aren't so sure anymore. It broke out a few more times, the last of them in sixteen-something, then just sort of disappeared. So if it *wasn't* bubonic plague, it's a whole new disease we've never tried antibiotics on, so they might work or they might not. And even if they did work, you'd have to move really, really fast and watch people, because if they caught it at night or something, they'd be dead before you'd think of giving them the pill. The early symptoms don't look serious, you see. The first thing that happens is you sneeze. Who'd think twice about that?" Her eyes were gleaming. "They made up a rhyme about it. You'll never guess what it was. . . ."

Michael said politely, "What was it?"

"'Ring a ring of roses, a pocketful of posies, a-tissue, a-tissue, we all fall down!'" She looked from one face to the other. "The old nursery rhyme is actually a plague song."

Opal came in then. All the color had drained from her face, and there was a frightened, haunted look in her eyes. "They're dead," she said. "Everybody's dead."

[13]

Danny, in Quarantine, Underground at Montauk

They ran together up the corridor, all four of them, to the entrance of their quarantine wing. Through the glass doors at the end they could see the bodies of their guards. One man was slumped with his back against a wall, head forward as if sleeping. The other was prostrate on the floor, his body bloated, sightless eyes staring upward at the ceiling. The skin of both men had taken on a bluish tinge, and there were swellings on their necks. It took only the briefest glance to confirm they were dead.

"Is it just the guards?" Michael asked, staring through the glass.

"No," Opal said. "There are other bodies just around the corner. I think everybody's dead."

"How do you know?" Danny asked.

"I went to look."

Michael said, "How did you get out?"

"The doors aren't locked anymore," Opal told him.

"How come?" Danny asked, frowning.

Without warning, Opal burst into tears. "I don't know. Does it matter? Look at them—they're dead! They were infected by whatever killed the colonel, and now they're dead."

Michael put his arms around her. "It's all right," he murmured.

"It's not all right!" Opal sobbed. "There are more bodies in the corridors. Doctors and nurses and . . . people, just people; and they look much worse than those two. And they all have this awful, terrified look on their faces."

"You went out and saw them?" Danny asked.

Opal pulled away from Michael and Fuchsia to round on him. "I didn't touch any of them, if that's what you're thinking. I don't have the disease."

"I was just thinking how brave you were," Danny told her.

Fuchsia said, "Of course you don't have the disease. None of us has it."

Opal stopped glaring at Danny to turn to Fuchsia. "Why do you think that?"

"It's what I was reading," Fuchsia explained. "The Black Death is terribly dangerous and you can catch it off somebody if they so much as breathe on you, but some people are naturally immune."

"You think we might be?" Michael asked.

"I think we must be," Fuchsia told him. "If we weren't immune, we'd be dead by now." She gave a weak version of her powerful smile. "It says in the book that anybody who came in contact with a plague victim would show symptoms within a few hours. Nearly everybody dies. In the Middle Ages there were putrefying corpses everywhere." She glanced through the glass doors. "Like those two."

"Are you sure we haven't been infected?" Danny asked.

"Hope not," Fuchsia said.

"You haven't," said a cool voice behind them.

[14]

Carradine, the Meeting Room, Montauk Underground Complex

It was almost funny, as if they were having a routine meeting like they did back in the old days. Except then the participants were mostly middle-aged. Here, Opal and Michael sat at one side of the table, Danny and Fuchsia at the other, while Carradine was at the head, middle-aged himself now. He felt ten years older than he had when he'd last seen them. In the mirror this morning, his skin was gray, his face taut with strain.

"You aren't going to die," Carradine said. He closed his eyes for a moment and gave a weak smile. "At least not from the disease." Michael opened his mouth, probably to ask for an explanation, but Carradine went on tiredly, "I'm sorry you had to . . . had to . . ." He let the sentence trail. What had happened was ghastly. What was worse was that his Project team was involved and about to get a lot more so, but he could see no way out of it. Which didn't mean he had to like it—they were only kids, for God's sake. Astral missions were one thing, but this . . . He collected his strength. "I'm sorry you had to see the bodies, find out this way what has happened. I should have been here to look out for you, but . . ."

But the whole thing had run out of control within hours, in spite of everything he'd tried to do to stop it. The trouble was, it had all sounded so far-fetched, like some second-rate disaster movie. Nobody took his demands for quarantine seriously until people started dying, and by then it was too late to save the base. And by the time the quarantine was imposed, he knew for certain there were one or two people who'd left Montauk. Nobody knew whether they'd contracted the disease or not, but if they had, the epidemic could go global within days, given the speed of modern air travel. He shrugged, paused, then said aloud, "This might easily turn into a worldwide crisis."

"Why aren't we going to die, Mr. Carradine?" Michael asked quietly.

He liked Michael. The boy never panicked, never made a fuss. "You've been vaccinated," Carradine told him. "So have I."

"Against bubonic plague?" Opal frowned. "I didn't think there was a vaccine."

"There is, as a matter of fact, but what we have here isn't bubonic plague."

They looked at him expectantly, and Fuchsia said, "So the Black Death *wasn't* bubonic plague?" She was the sharpest one of all, however she came across. If they could just find a way to switch on her talent fully, she'd be the best asset the Project had ever had.

"It isn't the Black Death either," Carradine told her.

"Then what is it?" Michael asked.

"It's complicated," Carradine said.

Fuchsia, who had a knack for getting to the heart of things, said, "Mr. Carradine, did you work on the original Montauk project—Project Rainbow?"

It was almost a relief to say yes. "It was back in the eighties," Carradine told them. "Not long after I joined the CIA as a young man. I was given the option of transfer to Montauk. They were short on details about what was going on here—need-to-know and all that—but it was obviously an important assignment, and I thought it would be good for my career, so I said yes. Even after I went to Montauk, it was nearly three months before I discovered they were involved in germ warfare."

There was a long moment's silence in the room before Danny exclaimed, "Bloody hell!"

"I thought biological warfare was outlawed," Opal said.

Carradine shrugged. "There was a Geneva Protocol as long ago as 1925 that banned the use of biological agents in warfare, but it didn't stop the Japanese from using them in China during World War Two. Then in 1972 America and the Soviets both signed the Biological Weapons Convention. That was a treaty prohibiting all biological weapons outright: production, stockpiling, or development. It also required the destruction of existing stockpiles. The trouble was, it was a treaty without teeth. No provision for inspection, no penalties for breaking it. The Soviets had had an active bioweapons program for years and so, frankly, had we. The difference was, we stopped ours after the treaty, and they didn't. They were still running theirs when the Soviet Union collapsed in 1991."

"But we didn't really stop ours, did we?" Opal asked mildly. "The American program, I mean."

Carradine sighed. "We did for a time. President Nixon held to the letter of the treaty for maybe a year, eighteen months. We even destroyed some of our stockpiles. But then the intelligence services began to accumulate evidence the Soviets were ignoring the agreement. What else could we do?"

"You started it all up again?" Danny asked, incredulous.

"What else could we do?"

"Mr. Carradine," Michael said, "what has this got to do with Montauk? I thought you told us Project Rainbow was about teleportation and time travel?"

Carradine had always thought of himself as a hard-bitten CIA man, who did what was necessary for the sake of the country and tried not to think too deeply about some of the consequences. But in the past he'd always been surrounded by fellow operatives who were just as hard-bitten. He took a deep breath. "You're too young to remember the Cold War. Two superpowers . . . the constant threat of nuclear Armageddon . . . proxy wars . . . the arms race . . . the Cuban Missile Crisis . . . America was the only country strong enough to stand up for democracy and freedom, and sometimes, in our enthusiasm, we made mistakes."

"Doesn't answer his question," Danny said.

Carradine said, "The official policy on germ warfare was to keep pace with the Soviets—just keep pace; no more than that. But there was a rogue element in the CIA who believed keeping pace would never be enough. They thought we needed *more* biological weapons than the Soviets, *better* biological weapons than the Soviets. They couldn't influence the number of weapons we had—not if they wanted to keep their activities secret—but they believed they *could* influence the quality."

"Quality?" Opal murmured. "You mean, how many people they could kill."

Carradine ignored her. "I'm afraid certain members of that rogue element infiltrated Montauk. Actually, what I should say is that the rogue element quietly took it over."

"What?" Danny asked. "Turned it into a germ warfare lab? Stopped messing around with time travel?"

"Nothing quite so obvious as that." Carradine shook his head. "And actually, time travel and germ warfare aren't a million miles apart."

Fuchsia's hand went up to her mouth. "Oh my God!" she exclaimed. "You don't mean—?"

Carradine nodded. "We had an operative, code-named Cobra, who wormed himself into a position where he was virtually running the practical operations at Montauk—not the whole project, not the admin, but the whole experimental side. This gave him and his team control of the time travel experiments, meant he could do more or less what he wanted and fake the reports if necessary." He hesitated, partly from reluctance, partly to see if the others had caught up, then said bluntly, "Cobra decided to investigate the possibility of using the Black Death in germ warfare."

"You mean he wanted to bring back Black Death samples from the Middle Ages or something?" Danny asked, eyes wide.

But Michael was frowning. "Why would he need

to? There've been recent outbreaks of bubonic plague in Asia."

"And I would imagine there are laboratory samples with the World Health Organization or somewhere," Opal said.

Carradine shook his head. "Actually, the Black Death *wasn't* bubonic plague, as Fuchsia seems to have guessed. Some scientists are beginning to suspect that from historical evidence, and I can confirm it. Bubonic plague is a bacterial infection. The Black Death was a filovirus like Ebola. But Cobra wasn't satisfied with that. He was obsessed with the idea of a mutation—something more virulent that would spread even more easily." He hesitated, then said, "Cobra used the Montauk time gate—quite illegally—to search history for that mutation. Now it looks as if he found it."

"You mean that's what was in the box?"

"I told you Project Rainbow ran into problems in 1988—all that was true and had nothing to do with the germ warfare activities, which were very much a black op. I also told you President Reagan closed the whole place down in 1989. What I didn't tell you was that it happened very quickly: Reagan was a decisive man. At the time we pulled the plug, Cobra was supposed to be on vacation. But that was just his cover. Only a handful of people knew he was actually on one of his time trips.

The thing was, we didn't know where, and there was no way to call him back. We couldn't even *try* to stop the closure without revealing what he'd been doing. All we could do was hope he got back in time. But he didn't. When the project closed, it left him trapped."

"Wow!" Danny exclaimed.

Carradine said, "The sample box that came through when we reactivated the machinery was identical to the ones we were using in the eighties. I wasn't expecting it, so I couldn't warn the colonel in time. When he opened it, some of the vials were broken, which meant the virus was loose inside. The colonel caught it at once. After that, it was too late."

"Back up a minute, Mr. Carradine," Danny cut in. "The rest of us were in that chamber too—how come we haven't all got it?"

Carradine smiled weakly. "That's where this meeting started. That's why I told you we weren't going to die of the plague." He sighed. "It's the only good thing to come out of this whole mess. When Cobra and his black-op team first planned their little field trips, they realized how potentially dangerous they would be. So the first step in their plan was to develop a supervaccine that would stimulate the immune system so strongly it would fight off *any* infection. To this day, only a hand-ful of CIA operatives know about the existence of that vaccine. I happen to be one of them. I've made sure it was included in the routine vaccinations of every active Shadow Project operative—a sort of atonement, I suppose. Have you noticed you haven't gotten sick since you joined the team?"

Opal was staring at him with a look that combined shock and bewilderment. "If you have a supervaccine, can't you use it to stop what's happening now?"

"I wish I could," Carradine told her. "First of all, a vaccine is designed to prevent a disease, not to cure it. Secondly, we don't have nearly enough supplies to vaccinate an entire population."

"Can't you make more?" Danny asked.

Carradine shook his head. "Not in time. The mass manufacture of any vaccine from its development stage takes about six months on average. This one contains some very rare ingredients, which would slow the process down even further. The existing stockpiles would protect a few hundred people at most. The virus is currently spreading like wildfire. A global pandemic is a day or two away at most."

"So there's nothing we can do?" Opal was beginning to panic. "This Cobra person has sent some sort of superbug through time to help the American germ warfare program, and now it's going to wipe out half the world?"

"That's about the size of it, but there *is* something you can do," Carradine said firmly. "If you're prepared to accept the mission, you can go back in time and stop Cobra before he sends through the doomsday box."

[15]

Carradine, the Meeting Room, Montauk Underground Complex

A ll of us?" Opal asked.

"Yes."

"Including you?"

Carradine shook his head. "I'll have to stay here and operate the time-gate machinery, otherwise you have no way of getting back."

Danny looked at him intently. "You want us to go back to the Middle Ages?"

They were moving toward the critical question already, and Carradine wasn't sure he was prepared to answer it. "I don't think so," he said simply.

But Danny, of course, wasn't going to leave it alone. "So how do we stop him?"

"Well," Carradine told them, "the first thing to say is that Cobra isn't a mad dog—he's not some sort of Joker character fighting Batman. He might be misguided, but he didn't plan to infect the world. So I figure—"

Fuchsia interrupted to ask, "What was Cobra's real name, Mr. Carradine?"

It was something he didn't want to get into at the moment. "He used different names. He spent most of his life undercover." He glared impatiently at Fuchsia. "Anyway, I figure what we need to do—what *you* need to do—is get to him *before* he sends through his little doomsday box, let him know the results of his actions, make sure he understands what will happen if he goes ahead. Once he realizes he's about to put the entire world in danger . . ." Carradine spread his hands. "As I said, he's not a mad dog. He'll never send the samples through after that."

Danny asked, "So you *do* want us to go back to the Middle Ages?"

Carradine shook his head. "Forget the Middle Ages, Danny. First off, we don't know where to find him in the Middle Ages—he could be anywhere from China to England—and we don't even know exactly *when*. Once the project closed, we lost our lock on him. Second thing is, if you *did* go to that time frame, you wouldn't survive a week. You don't have the right clothes; you couldn't even understand medieval English, let alone speak it. You don't know the customs of the period, don't know how to behave, don't have any money. You'd have to steal food or starve, and the second time they caught you, they'd hang you."

"What would they do the first time?" Danny asked.

"Cut your hand off," Carradine said bluntly.

Danny held up his hand and stared at it fondly.
"You've convinced me."

But apparently he hadn't convinced Opal, who said,
"Cobra managed to survive. Obviously."

"Cobra spent months—actually over a year—
preparing for his first trip to the fourteenth century. He
studied Middle English, Latin, and Old French. He read
social histories of the time. He had clothes specially made
in the style of the period. He had a purseful of genuine
coinage. He carried medieval weaponry—sword and a
dagger, as I recall—for his own protection . . . *and* he
could use it: he went through a course of special weapons
training. He had time to make his preparations and the
resources of the CIA behind him. We have neither. Just
about everybody at Montauk is dead or dying now, and
there's nobody on the outside riding to the rescue."

Danny shrugged. "So if it's not the Middle Ages,
then when?"

Carradine placed both palms on the tabletop and
leaned forward. "In theory, any time before he collects
the samples. In practice, it has to be a time period where
you can survive and move freely, where we know Cobra's
whereabouts, and ideally it should be a period where you

can find a little help when you need it. And believe me, you're going to need all the help you can get."

"You obviously have a time period in mind, Mr. Carradine," Michael said.

"The one year that checks all the boxes is 1962," Carradine told them. "Or at least most of them."

Opal echoed, "Nineteen sixty-two? Wouldn't it make more sense to send us back to 1988 or whenever it was, just before Cobra made his trip to the Middle Ages? We know where to find him—here at Montauk, obviously—and the whole plan would be fresh in his mind."

Carradine shook his head. "I'm afraid your chances of success here in the eighties would be as slim as your survival in the Middle Ages. What do you think would happen if the four of you turned up unannounced in a super-secret underground government project in the middle of the Cold War?"

"They'd cut our hands off?" Danny asked, deadpan.

"Maybe not, but it might take you a few years to get out of jail. Besides, even if you managed to reach Cobra, you have to remember he was in the middle of a black op, one he thought was vital for the future of the free world. He'd want to protect himself, and things could easily turn rough. At best, he wouldn't be very likely to believe you."

"Isn't that a problem whenever we meet up with

him?" Opal asked. "Not believing us, I mean?"

"Yes, it is. Frankly, I'd be far happier if we could pick a year closer to the time he got involved with the germ warfare thing, but I don't have access to CIA records at the moment, so I don't know where he was stationed at any given time. Except I happen to know he was at Langley in 1962 because his son was born that year. But sixty-two could be good, even though it isn't perfect. He was more open-minded in the sixties," Carradine said. "With the proper backup in sixty-two, he's likely to believe you." He hesitated. "I think."

Fuchsia hadn't spoken much. Now she did. "What do you mean by backup, Mr. Carradine?"

"We have a man in 1962." Carradine sighed. He'd already revealed so many official secrets, the big one hardly seemed to matter. "All right, here's the situation as I see it. You four may be working for the Shadow Project, but we're now in the world's greatest all-time god-awful mess, so I think I'm justified in officially co-opting you into the CIA. Project Rainbow was CIA, Cobra was CIA even though he was acting illegally, and it's up to the CIA to clean things up now, so I can justify that decision. As members of the CIA, you're bound by American secrecy laws just as tightly as you're already bound by the British Official Secrets Act. Pass on anything I've told you, anything I'm about to tell you, and you'll come out of jail about in time to draw your old-age pensions. Clear?"

"Clear," Michael said calmly. After a moment, the others murmured their assent.

"When we finally got a reliable time gate working at Montauk," Carradine went on, "senior management decided it would be a good idea to establish CIA stations at critical points of history. To keep an eye on things, so to speak, nudge events in the right direction. Obviously these stations had to be kept secret, so what most of them amounted to was one, maybe two agents in deep cover. Each functioned as our man on the spot in a particular time period. The CIA itself was set up in 1947 with headquarters in Washington. But in 1961, it transferred to Langley, Virginia. It was a hell of a move, lots of confusion, which gave us an opportunity to plant a temporal agent there: we had him safely in place by early sixty-two."

"You mean," Danny said incredulously, "the CIA infiltrated the *CIA*?"

"Essentially, yes," Carradine told him soberly. "We thought it was important to have him in place in the light of subsequent events. Where better than CIA headquarters, where he could pose as an ordinary agent and have access to the intelligence materials of his day? But the important thing is, the setup gives you a point of contact if you're looking for Cobra in 1962."

"I don't understand this, Mr. Carradine," Opal said.

"It's simple enough," Carradine told them. "I can send you to 1962, somewhere close to Langley. From there—"

Danny asked, "Why not into Langley itself, since that's obviously where we're going?"

"There's no way we want you appearing suddenly where you're likely to be seen—people would start to ask too many questions," Carradine explained. "Standard procedure is to transport you to a remote spot within reach of your ultimate target. You make your way from there. Once you reach Langley, I want you to go directly to CIA headquarters. When you get there, ask for Jack Stratford. You got that name?"

"Jack Stratford," Michael murmured.

"Since you've no valid credentials, he'll refuse to see you. At that point, you should instruct the receptionist to give him this." He tossed a folded slip of paper onto the table. Opal picked it up and hesitantly opened it. The others leaned forward to see. On the paper was written the single word *Chronos*. "Then leave and make your way to Pete's Pies and Coffee. It's only a couple of blocks away; anybody will give you directions. Order yourselves coffees and anything else you want. Jack Stratford will join you inside fifteen minutes and pay the bill."

"Jack Stratford is our man in 1962, right?" Danny put in.

"Right," Carradine confirmed.

"What happens then?" Opal asked.

"Stratford will set you up to function in 1962, provide you with everything you need for your mission." He hesitated, then added, "Providing you're willing to undertake it."

[16]

Danny, the Meeting Room, Montauk Underground Complex

"Okay," said Carradine briskly when the rest of the briefing was finished, "get back to your individual quarters and get yourselves ready, then join me in the transportation chamber." He caught the blank looks and added, "Where you saw the time gate: we called it the transportation chamber. For obvious reasons." As they pushed their chairs back, he said casually, "Danny, would you hold up a minute?"

"Sure."

As the door closed behind the others, Carradine said thoughtfully to Danny, "You were brought up in a particularly rough area of London—right?"

"Rough enough," Danny muttered tersely. He disliked talking about his past, even though he was aware Carradine knew all about it from his file. The question was, why was Carradine bringing it up now?

"Must have met some hard men," Carradine said.

"A few." Danny watched him suspiciously, wondering where this was going.

Carradine parked his backside on the edge of the conference table, the picture of relaxed confidence. Except he was neither relaxed, nor particularly confident. If Danny was reading him right, the casual pose was just an act. There was something on Carradine's mind. Danny waited. Carradine glanced toward the strip light in the ceiling, looked back at Danny, then asked, "How did you deal with them?"

"Kept out of their way, mostly."

"And when you couldn't keep out of their way?"

Danny took a deep breath. "What are you asking me, Mr. Carradine? What are you asking me *really*?"

"Ever use a knife?"

"*Cripes, Mr. Carradine!* What's this about?"

Carradine licked his lips. "Did it occur to you to wonder what will happen if we can't persuade Cobra to abandon his plans?"

"Sure it did. But you said he's not a mad dog."

"He's not. He's not going to send the samples if they lead to the deaths of millions of Americans. I'm certain of that. What worries me is that he may not believe us."

"That we've come from the future?" Danny asked. He supposed it did sound a bit far-fetched.

Carradine shook his head. "That could be tricky,

all right, although I think the chances are he'll buy it. The Montauk complex wasn't built until 1967, but by sixty-two Cobra would have heard rumors about Project Rainbow, even though he wasn't working for it then. No, my worry is the time element. We're asking him to commit to something that won't happen for more than twenty years. Think about it, Danny. I ask you to do something in twenty years' time and you could be happy to promise today, but you've got two decades to change your mind. You're a different person in twenty years. And even if he accepts your approach as genuine, he may not believe what we tell him about the outcome of his germ warfare mission."

"Why wouldn't he believe us? Why would we go to the trouble of traveling through time"—and speaking of belief, Danny couldn't believe he'd just said that—"to tell him lies?"

"You could be working for the Russians. Or the Chinese. Or somebody who wanted to sabotage America's biological weapons program."

"What about your note?"

"I could be working for the Russians too."

"So he may not trust you either?"

Carradine shrugged. "This is the CIA. We're trained not to trust anybody."

Danny stared at Mr. Carradine briefly, then said,

"When you were talking to us, when you were telling us about Cobra, you kept saying *we*. Like, *we did this* and *we did that*."

Carradine stiffened visibly. "What's your point, Danny?"

"You seemed to know an awful lot about it. I was wondering if you were part of it."

"Part of what?"

"Part of Cobra's nasty little undercover team. You said there were others involved. Were you one of them?"

He thought Mr. Carradine might get angry, but all that happened was he stayed silent for a long moment, then said slowly, "No, Danny. No, I wasn't. I didn't agree with what they were doing and I wasn't a member of the black-op team."

"But you knew what they were up to?"

"Yes."

"In detail?"

"Yes."

"Why didn't you blow the whistle on them?"

To his astonishment, Mr. Carradine gave a wan smile. "Good question, Danny."

"What's the answer?" Danny pushed.

Carradine said, "Agent Cobra is my father."

Danny suddenly became aware of his heartbeat, ticking off the seconds. Eventually he said, "I'm sorry."

Carradine sighed. "I suppose I should have come clean right at the start. You can tell the others when you see them. Or not. I don't suppose it matters, really. I was just . . . You know, it was just that . . ."

It had been a while since Danny felt sorry for anybody in authority, but he felt sorry for Mr. Carradine now. "I understand," he said. "Blood thicker than water and all that, never mind the regulations." Frankly, he'd have done the same if Cobra had been his old Nan.

"I let him go too far. I know that now. But we all have twenty-twenty hindsight." He slid one hand into his jacket pocket. "Danny," he said, "you're different from the others. They've never had to survive among the lowlifes like you did. You couldn't trust them with something like this, could you?"

"Something like what?" Danny asked.

"Danny," Carradine said. "I want you to do your best to persuade Cobra—your very best. But if you can't persuade him, or even if you have any doubt in your mind that he's really, genuinely persuaded, I want you to kill him."

Danny stared, saying nothing.

"You can do the math, Danny. If Cobra sends the samples through, millions die. One life; millions of lives."

Danny still didn't speak.

"You're the only one capable," Carradine said. "The

others couldn't. I wouldn't even ask them. But you're a realist. You'll know if it has to be done."

Danny felt so cold inside he was positively numb. Suddenly he found his voice and, to his intense surprise, it sounded calm. "You're wrong, Mr. Carradine. I couldn't do it either."

It was as if Carradine hadn't heard him. He drew his hand from his jacket pocket, and Danny saw it was holding a small, scuffed, leather-covered box, looking for all the world as if it might contain an engagement ring. "I want you to take this," Carradine said, holding it out to him.

"What is it?" Danny asked suspiciously. He drew away from the outstretched hand. Somehow he didn't think this was a marriage proposal.

Carradine flicked the box open with his thumb. Inside, nestling on the worn velvet padding, was an antique gold ring set with a large polished amethyst. He put the box down and took out the ring. "See this catch?" He used his thumbnail to press on what looked like a decoration in the setting. The amethyst sprang open like a lid, revealing a depression filled with powdery white crystals. A faint smell of almonds filled the air. "Two hundred fifty milligrams of potassium cyanide," Carradine said. "It's what the Nazis used to kill themselves after the war. Fastest-acting poison known.

Swallow this and you'll collapse immediately. You'll lose consciousness in ten to twenty seconds. A minute or so after that and you're dead from cardiac arrest." He pressed down to close up the amethyst. "It's soluble in alcohol or water, or you can sprinkle it on food."

Danny stared at the ring in horrified fascination. "You want me to feed this poison to your father?"

"Hopefully you won't have to," Carradine said. "I pray to God you won't have to. But there are millions of lives at stake. Literally millions. Call it insurance."

Danny had started to feel sick to his stomach, sick and dizzy. "You're asking me to kill *your own father!*" he hissed.

"Take the ring," Carradine said quietly. "You don't have to tell the others if you don't want to. Just take the ring. You decide when to use it, if ever. Your decision, absolutely. And only if you're sure—*you're* sure, nobody else—there is absolutely no other way. Insurance, like I said. Take it, Danny."

Danny watched his own hand reach out to take the ring.

[17]

Fuchsia, the Transportation Chamber, the Montauk Project

The equipment was sort of retro—all eighties brushed aluminum and banks of sliders—but sort of futuristic too. Mr. Carradine had switched on the power, and the chamber was filled with a gentle hum.

The others were already there. Michael looked okay, which could just be because he hid his feelings so well. Opal looked nervous, like you'd expect, but Danny was looking positively sick. He was a much more sensitive soul than he pretended, and he was probably worried about what would happen if they couldn't complete their mission. All those people dead from some horrible germ warfare mutation: it was a huge responsibility. Although oddly enough, Fuchsia wasn't afraid, because she had a good feeling about the mission. Not one of her actual *flashes*, but just a generalized good feeling, as if everything was going to be all right.

She moved across to stand beside Danny. "Are you okay?" she whispered.

"Yes. Yes, I'm fine."

The control equipment seemed to take the raw edge off the rift, so that it no longer looked like an impossible void leading into nothingness. Fuchsia was glad of that: it made the whole thing less scary. She wondered what the sensation of traveling through time would be like. It was actually really hard to imagine. The sensation of traveling through space varied from nothing much when you were taking a walk, to really exciting when you were riding a roller coaster. Maybe traveling through time was something like that: it depended on how fast you went and how far. Or maybe it wasn't. But she'd soon find out.

"Everybody ready?" Mr. Carradine asked in that sort of hearty, *Everything's under control and perfectly all right* voice adults seemed to put on when they were worried sick.

They all muttered yes. All the same, he asked, "Got the packs I made up for you?"

They nodded. The packs were wallets of maps and things to help them until they got to Mr. Stratford. Not much to be taking on a time trip. Not even an overnight case with a change of underwear and toothbrush, but Mr. Stratford was supposed to arrange everything for them so there would be no anachronisms—nothing out of place in 1962.

"All wearing your badges?"

Again the collective murmur of assent. The badges, Mr. Carradine had explained, were actually miniaturized communications devices that would be used to report the completion of their mission.

"Okay," Carradine said. "Let's get started—and good luck." He pushed three of the sliders, and the hum in the chamber racked up quickly into a high-pitched whine. To Fuchsia's surprise, the rift between the two huge magnets changed color and began to emit a pleasing violet glow.

"That's pretty," she murmured.

Mr. Carradine glanced across at her. "Matter-antimatter collisions generate violet photons," he told her.

"Cool," Fuchsia said.

"So what do we do now?" Michael asked.

"I'd like to send all of you together," Carradine said. "It's a bit safer that way. If you send people sequentially— one after the other—there's the risk of slight variations in the particle flow. When that happens, it means you all arrive at different times. It's usually only a matter of seconds, or minutes at most, but it can sometimes be as much as an hour or two, which would be confusing and inconvenient. I'd rather send you together if you can all fit between the pillars."

"I imagine we can," Michael told him.

"We'll snuggle up close," Fuchsia said to Danny, grinning. She reached out and took his hand. She noticed Michael had already taken Opal's, which was nice. They walked forward and stood between the magnetic pillars. There was, in fact, plenty of room for all four of them.

"Okay," Carradine said. "Here we go!" He made some final adjustments and threw a switch. The hum that had become a whine increased in volume, then went off the scale. The lights in the chamber flickered, then their whole environment dissolved into a maelstrom of conflicting energies.

Just before she blacked out, Fuchsia suddenly felt uneasy.

[18]

The Team, Somewhere in America, 1962

This can't be right," Opal said, frowning.

She and Danny were standing with Michael and Fuchsia in what looked like a well-tended garden, or possibly a park. The sun was shining, in stark contrast to the harsh strip lights in the Montauk complex, and the grass underfoot had more the look of a lawn than a meadow. They had materialized—there was no other word for it—between two large, sheltering bushes, and emerged, after momentary disorientation, onto a narrow path beside a flower bed.

"I thought we'd be in a city," Opal said. "Isn't Langley—?"

"Mr. Carradine wanted us to arrive somewhere we wouldn't be seen," Michael told her.

"I know, but I thought that meant a back alley or an empty room or something."

From the corner of his eye, Danny noticed that

Fuchsia, still in the shelter of the bushes, was bent over as if she was about to be sick. "Are you all right?" he asked urgently.

Fuchsia raised her head and looked into his face with an expression of bewilderment. Her eyes were round and the pupils dilated. "Everything's all wrong," she whispered. "I don't see you properly."

"What, like I'm blurred?"

Fuchsia shook her head. "I didn't say I couldn't see you. It's more that I'm not seeing you properly. It's as if you're stretched out, like a worm. Actually *everything* looks stretched out."

"Look, maybe you'd better sit down." He reached out to take her arm. "Fuchsia's not feeling well," he called to the others.

Opal came over at once and put her arm around Fuchsia's shoulders. "Are you going to be sick?"

"It may be a reaction to time travel," Michael remarked. "I found it a bit disorienting myself."

"Me too," Danny said. But the feeling had passed quickly. He looked worriedly at Fuchsia, wondering what they would do if she really *was* sick with a bug or something. Did they have antibiotics in 1962?

"I'm not ill," Fuchsia said. "I'm different."

"What way different?" Opal asked her gently.

"It's the way I see things." She screwed her eyes tight

shut, then opened them again. "That's better. A bit. Maybe if I . . ." She did the eye thing again. "That's nearly normal."

"This isn't to do with your precog talent, is it?" Michael asked her.

"Yes," Fuchsia said. "Yes, I think it is. It's as if something's changed it."

Opal said, "Mr. Carradine never really told the rest of us much about you. What exactly is your talent? Or can't you talk about it?"

"Oh, it's not a secret or anything—it's just that there hasn't been much to talk about. I'm not special like the rest of you: I couldn't leave my body even when they tried me with the helmet. But ever since I was a little girl, I've had these weird feelings about things that were going to happen, and some of them came true. When I turned twelve, I started to get blackouts, and the doctor couldn't find a reason. And actually they weren't blackouts, not really: I saw visions, flashes—"

"Flashes of the future?" Michael asked.

"Yes," Fuchsia said matter-of-factly. "Only some of them didn't come true—"

"But some did?" Michael interrupted again.

"Oh, yes, of course. Actually most of them did, although there weren't very many. And there were some blackouts where I didn't remember anything afterward but I talked during them and described things, and my father wrote them down. He's a university professor and he wanted to have me properly tested at Edinburgh— they have a parapsychology department there. But then the Shadow Project got wind of it and recruited me for training. Except that the training hasn't worked very well up to now. But the strange thing—" She stopped, staring into the middle distance.

"What's the strange thing, Fuchsia?" Danny prompted her.

"Just now," Fuchsia said, "when you thought I was being sick, I was seeing the future, but not in flashes like I used to."

"Can you describe it?" Danny asked. He was starting to feel excited. It wasn't every day you found somebody who could see the future.

"I think I can bring it back," Fuchsia said. She closed her eyes and jerked her head sharply, like a nervous twitch. She opened her eyes briefly. "Nearly." She shut them again and gave another twitch. "Got it!" she exclaimed as she opened her eyes again. She stared around her as if examining the scene for the first time, then slowly smiled. "This is cool!" The smile disappeared. "Losing it . . ." She turned back to Danny. "Gone."

"What did you have? A picture of the future?"

"Yes, sort of," Fuchsia said. "Just for a second, but I

definitely had it. I think with practice I might be able to hold it longer, maybe turn it on and off when I want." She looked at them, wide-eyed. "It's not at all like I expected."

Opal said, "What's it like, Fuchsia?"

"It's as if I can see time."

Danny pushed in again. "You can *see* time?"

"What's it like?" Michael asked.

"It's like looking across a broad plain and there are roads running through it. Only some of the roads are misty and not quite there, but others are very solid and real. Does that make sense to you?"

"Not a lot," Danny said.

"Look," said Opal gently, "we can talk about this later. If you're really all right, Fuchsia?"

Fuchsia grinned. "Yes, definitely. And I'd like to think about it anyway."

"The thing is," Opal said, "we need to find our way to Langley and meet up with Agent Stratford, and I'm not sure I know exactly how to do that. Where are we? Does anybody know?"

"Have you looked at your map? There's one in the packs Mr. Carradine gave us."

"Yes, I have," Opal said. She produced her map. "I think we may be on the George Washington Memorial Parkway, but I can't find Langley anywhere."

"Can you find McLean?" Michael asked.

Opal peered at her map. "Yes, it's to the left of the parkway."

"That's Langley," Michael said. "At least, Langley's a part of McLean. A neighborhood, as they call it over here."

Opal folded her map. "All right, we think we know where we are now, but how do we get ourselves to Langley and CIA headquarters?"

Fuchsia said, a little hazily, "We take the bus that's coming any minute. It will drop us at the gate."

[19]

Danny and the Team, CIA Headquarters, Langley, 1962

CIA headquarters at Langley was a new-looking, flat-roofed, pale-colored building fronted by a stretch of well-kept lawn. It looked more like a university campus than the home of the country's most important intelligence service.

"How did you do that?" Danny asked Fuchsia quietly as they walked into the enormous lobby.

"Do what?"

"The bus. How did you know it was coming? How did you know it would get us here?"

Fuchsia grinned a little smugly. "I could see it coming and us riding in it."

Danny decided to leave the questions until they had a bit more time together. But however confused he felt just now, one thing was sure: using the time gate at Montauk seemed to have stimulated Fuchsia's precog ability and even given her some control over it. That was going to be very useful. Very useful indeed.

There was a biblical quotation at the entrance to the lobby: AND YE SHALL KNOW THE TRUTH AND THE TRUTH SHALL MAKE YOU FREE—JOHN VIII.XXXII. The lobby itself was dominated by an enormous circular granite seal, which must have been easily sixteen feet in diameter, inlaid into the flooring. It showed an eagle's head above a shield with a sixteen-pointed star in the middle. Around the outer circle were the words *Central Intelligence Agency United States of America.*

Danny was still staring around foolishly when Michael took him by the arm. "Come on, there's a reception desk over there. The girls are on their way."

"Does Opal have the note for Agent Stratford?"

Michael nodded. "She put it in an envelope."

"I don't like this arrangement," Danny said. "Suppose he doesn't come for us at the coffee place? We'll be stuck in 1962 with nowhere to go and no way of completing our mission." He didn't like the thought of problems on their mission. He had enough to worry about already. The ring box was weighing heavily in his pocket, and he couldn't get Mr. Carradine's words out of his head.

"It's the only arrangement we have," Michael told him coolly. "So let's not worry about things going wrong until it actually happens. And by the way, I wouldn't say things like 'stuck in 1962' too often. If you're overheard, it might start people wondering."

Danny bit back a sharp retort, mainly because he couldn't think of one. They caught up with the girls just as they reached the desk. A uniformed receptionist stared at them without noticeable warmth, probably wondering what sort of nuisances four teenagers would turn out to be. Opal, who never seemed intimidated by anyone, said firmly, "We're here to see Agent Jack Stratford, please."

The receptionist flipped quickly through a card index on the right of the desk. "Is he expecting you?"

"I don't know," said Opal bluntly. She held the woman's gaze.

"What are your names, please?"

"I'm Opal Harrington; this is Fuchsia Benson, Michael Potolo, and Danny Lipman."

"What is the nature of your business with Agent Stratford?"

To Danny's delight, Opal said calmly, "That information is classified."

The receptionist gave them a long-suffering look, and it occurred to Danny that jokers must use that line on her all the time. But all she said was "Do you have personal identification?"

Opal shook her head. "I'm afraid not."

"Then I can't disturb Agent Stratford." She gave

Opal a frosty smile. "If you'd like to come back with personal ID . . ."

Danny loved the way Opal handled herself in situations like this. He watched now to see what she would do. What she did do was drop a small white envelope onto the reception desk. "Perhaps you could ensure this reaches Agent Stratford as soon as possible," she said. Then, without waiting for a response, she turned and walked away, signaling the others to follow with a small flick of her head.

"Do you think she'll give it to him?" Danny asked as they headed for the doors.

"Hope so," Opal told him calmly.

"What happens if she doesn't?"

"We go to Plan B."

"What's Plan B?" Danny asked.

"Haven't you worked it out yet?" Opal grinned at him suddenly. "I feel a bit relieved, actually. We've done exactly what Mr. Carradine asked us to, and it went exactly as he said it would. Now all we have to do is find Pete's Pies."

Pete's Pies and Coffee turned out to be one of those typical American diners they'd seen so often in movies. There were tables set along a window that looked onto the street, and a bar with stools where you could watch your order being plated. They commandeered a table by the window with some vague thought of watching out for Agent Stratford, even though they had no idea what he looked like. A waitress appeared, and they all ordered coffees except Danny, who insisted on a supersize slice of apple pie with a double helping of whipped cream.

"What?" he demanded when they stared at him. "I'm nervous, all right? I always eat when I'm nervous."

"We don't have very much money, Danny," Opal whispered, as the waitress departed. In fact they had almost none. Mr. Carradine had had no way of supplying them with 1962 banknotes, so they were making do with a handful of coins. None of these was 1962 vintage either, but he'd assured them no one ever checked dates on a coin so long as it looked and felt right. But their little hoard was depleted by their bus fares, and at five cents the apple pie was one of the more expensive items on the menu.

"Carradine said this Stratford character will pick up the bill," Danny muttered as he tucked into his pie.

"Let's hope he arrives before they give it to us," Opal told him.

In fact, the predicted fifteen minutes came and went with no sign of Agent Stratford. After half an hour, the talk among the group shifted from worrying about the bill ("We can always leg it without paying," Danny said. "Not the first time I've had to.") to speculating about what Stratford looked like.

"He's a CIA agent," Fuchsia said. "He's bound to be tall and handsome, like Mr. Carradine."

"Do you think Mr. Carradine is handsome?" Opal asked, surprised.

Fuchsia nodded enthusiastically. "I think he looks like Nicolas Cage."

They were still discussing Carradine when a short, plump man in a rumpled suit materialized beside their table. "You the Chronos kids?" he asked in a strong Bronx accent. "I'm Jack Stratford."

[20]

Opal, McLean, 1962

They'd expected to go back to CIA headquarters, but Agent Stratford took them shopping instead. "You stick out like sore thumbs in that gear," he told them. "You girls are wearing *pants*, for chrissake!" He looked at Fuchsia. "You're even wearing trousers and a skirt. I know kids like to dress batty, but I'm not just talking fashion statements here. Some of your clothes are made from stuff that hasn't even been invented yet. You want people asking questions?"

Stratford's car was one of those monsters with fins that did about five miles to the gallon. "Best you go in the back and keep your head down," Stratford said to Michael. "Johnson won't sign the Civil Rights Act for a couple of years, so you'd attract attention being driven by a white man. Sorry about that."

"Hardly your fault," Michael said calmly. He climbed into the back of the car and slid across the leather upholstery. Danny climbed in beside him while both girls sat up front.

"Okay," Stratford said as they headed into town, "as I understand it, you're looking for one of our field agents, code-named Cobra. This is your first time mission. You've had no CIA training and precious little preparation, but you've done stuff for our Limey cousins and you do have some very spooky talents the nature of which is classified information. That about it?"

Opal looked at him with surprise. "How did you know all that?" A thought occurred to her, and she asked, "Are you in touch with Mr. Carradine?"

"Your controller back in your own time? Naw, the energy requirements for verbal communication through time are off the scale. Even those little badges of yours are costly to run, and all they do is send a microsecond beep to signal the end of your mission."

"So how did you know?"

"It was all on the piece of paper you sent me."

Opal stared at him for a moment, frowning. "Agent Stratford—"

"Jack. Call me Jack."

"Agent Stratford," Opal repeated, "there was nothing on that piece of paper except the one word *Chronos*."

"That's true," Danny murmured from the backseat.

"Call yourselves spies? Carradine sent a full briefing.

Only the ink was invisible."

Danny stared at him in astonishment. "You mean like lemon juice? I used to do that when I was a boy. Once it dries you have to heat it before you can see it."

"Bit more sophisticated that that, kid." Stratford sniffed. "It's a special mix and a special spray to make it visible. The word you can see—*Chronos*—tells me you're time travelers and I should take the message seriously. The spray brings up the message itself. Any consolation, I have to render you all and any assistance." He pulled the car over and parked outside a department store. "Okay, let's get you into some sensible clothes."

The clothes turned out to be more cute than sensible. Fuchsia had been hoping for something really colorful with flowers, but the hippie movement obviously hadn't started up yet, and both she and Opal ended up in what was more like fifties gear—tight sweaters and wide skirts with lots of petticoats. The boys weren't much better off. Mr. Stratford equipped them with tapered pants, matching jackets, shirts, and ties, and muttered something about shorter haircuts. Michael looked cool and conservative—but then he always did. Danny managed to break the mold a little by insisting on a black shirt with a white tie, but all it really did was make him look as if he'd joined the Mafia. Stratford pronounced himself satisfied, however. They could now pass for early-sixties teens without attracting too much attention.

"Where to now, Mr. Stratford?" Opal asked as they climbed back into the car.

"Bank," Stratford told them tersely. "Then I gotta organize a place for you to stay."

The place to stay turned out to be a brownstone in a leafy suburb, bigger on the inside than it looked from the street. Stratford showed them into a well-appointed living room. "Okay," he said, "this is a CIA safe house. I've requisitioned it for the duration of your mission, so the good news is you're not likely to be disturbed. The bad news is you'll have to fend for yourselves—cooking, cleaning, shopping—and don't think you can get away with leaving it a mess when you're finished, because the CIA has ways of dealing with sloppy teenagers."

"It's all right," Opal said. "We're mostly English."

Stratford gave her a look, then went on, "Fridge is stocked, so are the kitchen cupboards. Try to replace anything you use."

"Actually, Mr. Strat—" She hesitated. "Actually, Jack, we may have difficulty replacing things: we don't have much money. Mr. Carradine said—"

"I know, I know. He said I'd organize a float for you. Every Chronos agent gets around to that sooner or later; usually sooner." He walked across to a table in the corner of the room. "Okay, gather 'round and see what your

Uncle Jack brought you home from the bank." He began to pull bundles of dollars from his jacket pockets. Danny watched wide-eyed as he tossed them down. "I'd suggest you store some here for emergencies—there's a safe behind the picture. There's nothing bigger than a dollar bill here, but don't forget you get more bang for your buck in this time than you're used to. But let me tell you two things. One, you don't flash your money around. Ever. That's the best way to get yourself noticed, and getting yourself noticed is the best way of getting into trouble. Two, you're accountable because I'm accountable, so don't sweat the small stuff, but I'll be looking for receipts on any big expenditures when your mission is over. Clear?"

"Makes sense," Danny said. "But what's the deal with us and the rest of the CIA? I mean, if you're not around, can we walk in and get more cash if we need it?"

"No, you cannot," Stratford said firmly. "The deal is you work through me or not at all. Also, you do not, repeat *not*, reveal my identity as a temporal agent. Or yours, for that matter. If you have any reason to contact me at headquarters, I'm plain Agent Stratford. I work for the CIA in a fairly senior capacity, but I was recruited in the usual way two years after I graduated. My files back up the whole cover story. Any one of you so much as hint I'm not what I seem or mention time travel, I'll order a psychiatric evaluation on all four of you. You wouldn't want that. They still do lobotomies on mental patients in this era."

Danny grinned at him. "I get the picture."

Michael said, much more soberly, "We understand, Mr. Stratford. You can rely on our discretion."

Opal was still standing by the table. She had picked up one of the banded stacks of bills and was riffling through it. "Actually, Agent Stratford, I don't think we're going to need all this money, or anything like it. If Mr. Carradine briefed you with the invisible-ink thing, you'll know all we have to do is make direct contact with another CIA agent who's currently at Langley."

"That's right—Cobra," Stratford said.

Opal said, "We're hoping you can find out what name he's currently operating under, track him down at Langley, then get us an introduction. We just need to talk to him for half an hour. After that, the mission's finished and we signal to Mr. Carradine to bring us . . . home." Her voice trailed away. "What? What is it, Mr. Stratford?"

Stratford licked his lips, and a pained expression crossed his features. "That's the thing, see? When I got Carradine's briefing, I thought I'd save a little time by tracking Cobra down. That's why I was late at the diner. Cobra's a code name, of course, but I found out that, day to day, he operates as Robert Mendez, although that may not be his real name. I don't know what rank he holds in your time, but this year he's working as a covert field agent." He took a deep breath.

"But this is brilliant, Mr. Stratford," Opal exclaimed. "All you have to do now is take us to him. We probably won't even need to use this house."

"Yes, you will," Stratford said. "Carradine was wrong about one thing, see? Cobra isn't at Langley. He's currently in Moscow. If you want to talk to him, you'll have to travel to the USSR."

[21]

Michael, Safe House, McLean, Virginia, 1962

We can't travel to the USSR!" Danny gasped.

Michael glanced at him in surprise. Danny usually took problems in his stride and was game for more or less anything. But now he'd actually gone pale. All the same . . . "I'm afraid Danny may be right, Mr. Stratford." He looked around at the others. "Do any of you speak Russian? I certainly don't." They shook their heads.

"You won't reach the USSR without help, that's for sure," Stratford said. "How important is your mission?"

"Very," Opal said promptly. "It has to do with—"

Stratford held up his hand quickly. "No details. I'm carrying enough secrets already, and yours I don't need to know. What I'm asking is whether it's worth taking risks. Like you said, everybody expected you'd meet up with Cobra in a nice comfy office at Langley and chat with him for half an hour, then go home. Everybody including your controller. What I'm asking is, would

Mr. Carradine expect you to put yourselves in danger to complete this mission?"

They looked at one another, turned back to Stratford, and slowly nodded. Even Danny reluctantly agreed.

"Okay," Stratford said. "Then we got a situation here. To complete your mission, you have to go to Russia. But you can't just climb on a plane and fly to Moscow. This is 1962, and the Cold War looks like hell freezing over. Russia isn't exactly a tourist trap. You'll need papers, special visas. I can probably get you over there, but frankly that's only the start of your problems. Any of you will be marked the minute you get into the country. Walk down the street to buy your morning paper and you're under KGB surveillance. Talk to the wrong people, make a suspicious move, and they'll haul your butts into jail. Cobra's working undercover in Moscow, I can tell you that, but I can't tell you where to find him yet. Tracking him down would be difficult for an experienced Russia hand. For four kids who haven't been there before—you haven't, have you? Thought not—it's going to be close to impossible."

Opal said, a little frostily, "You keep calling us kids, Agent Stratford, but we do have some espionage experience."

"Yeah, I know, and I know you aren't kids really, but you're not middle-aged men and women either, and since you're operating on your own, believe me, you're going to attract even more attention than the average Westerner, and they get plenty."

"What's your situation, Mr. Stratford?" Michael asked suddenly.

"What do you mean, what's my situation?"

"Mr. Carradine described you as 'our man in 1962.' So while you appear to be working for the CIA in this time period, you're actually working for Project Rainbow, am I right?"

Stratford gave a small smile. "Not just Rainbow. If you don't know this already, I never mentioned it, but Rainbow's only part of a whole secret CIA operation. What are you getting at, Mike?"

"I'm just trying to be clear," Michael said. "Do I take it that apart from your work as a time agent—for Project Rainbow or whatever—you function as a normal CIA agent in this time frame?"

"As a cover, yeah."

"So you have access to CIA backup, even though the CIA in 1962 might not know you're using it to do your job as a time agent?"

"You know I do, Mike." Stratford nodded toward the table. "Where do you think that cash came from—my salary? Or this house? I told you this was a CIA safe house."

Before Michael could say anything else, Opal put

in quickly, "We're very grateful, Mr. Stratford, we really are. And I'm sure Mr. Carradine would want us to press on. You think you can arrange papers and get us on a flight to Moscow?"

"Not a direct flight," Stratford said. "Don't have them in 1962. You'll have to go via London, but that's okay. What I have in mind is to get you to the American embassy in Moscow. If you're embassy kids you'll be closely watched, but you'd be closely watched anyway, and you'll be a bit safer if you're known to have official backing. Besides, it will give you somewhere to live and protection if things go wrong, assuming you can get back to the embassy building. You'll need a cover story for the ambassador, but we'll work that out. You'll need papers, like we said, but I can get those forged for you by this time tomorrow."

"We're British," Danny said suddenly. "They'll know we're not Americans the minute we open our mouths."

"I thought of making it the British embassy," Stratford said. "Could probably arrange that, but it's going to take a lot more time."

"I'm not sure we have a lot more time," Opal told him.

"Listen," Stratford said firmly, "neither embassy is perfect, but on balance you'll be better off in the U.S. embassy. Pretend you're Americans educated in England or call yourselves Brits. Won't matter. Heck, we're supposed to be allies, aren't we? Think the Russians will care? Embassy staff won't either, 'specially if you keep to yourselves as much as possible. The ambassador will know you're agents, so nobody's going to make a fuss."

"Time agents?" Michael asked.

"No, not *time* agents. I already told you, that's the one secret you take to your graves, pardon the expression. You'll be CIA special agents on a special CIA mission with me as your official controller. That's all the ambassador needs to know, all he will know. This doesn't have to be a James Bond mission. If you work it right, we get you into Russia, you find Cobra, have your little chat, then we get you out again, nobody any the wiser; no fuss, no muss."

"How do we find Cobra?" Opal asked.

"Leave that to me, Miss Harrington," Stratford said. "I'll try to help you any way I can. He's undercover, so it won't be easy, but I should be able to set up a meeting for you by the time you get to Moscow."

"I suppose it would be against the rules if you came with us?" Michael asked him suddenly.

Stratford shook his head. "You'll want to move as fast as possible, and I have stuff I have to do here. You're on your own. But I can teach you some tricks of the trade before you go."

"What sort of tricks?" Michael asked, suddenly curious.

"How to lose surveillance when the KGB starts tailing you might be useful," Stratford said. "One or two other simple bits and pieces." He peeled off his jacket and hung it over the back of a chair. "Let's get started."

[22]

Danny, 31,000 Feet over Sweden, 1962

Danny knew he would die within the next five minutes. Flying London to New York in a modern jet had been bad enough, but the 1962 Aeroflot plane from London to Moscow looked like it might have been tied together with string. The seats needed cleaning, the flight attendants were thick-set and brooding—although probably great at tramping to civilization across a snowfield when the plane actually crashed. One really strange detail, though, was that the meals were served with sterling silver cutlery in place of the usual plastic knives and forks. Not that Danny had any appetite. The food was disgusting, and a combination of fear and worry locked his stomach. Not that it mattered. In five minutes, max, the plane would drop out of the sky and all his worries would be over. He wondered vaguely if he'd spend the afterlife in his astral body.

The engine gave a brief, disturbing howl as Fuchsia

slipped into the seat beside him. The scary flight attendants had allocated each of them separate seats because of the numbering on their tickets even though the flight was almost empty. Danny—and the others, presumably—had even been told by a uniformed woman who looked like a wrestler that it was "forbidden by regulations" to change seats. But now the flight attendants had all moved to the back of the plane. None of them was looking at the passengers when Fuchsia seized her chance.

"Are you all right, Danny?" Fuchsia asked anxiously. "I know you don't like flying."

"Fine," Danny muttered through clenched teeth. "Glad to see you, though."

"Yes, I know," Fuchsia said. She settled into the seat. "Wasn't the food ghastly?"

It was the perfect opportunity. He'd wanted to talk to her earlier, but it had proved incredibly difficult to get her alone. Now . . . Danny licked his lips. "I want you to do me a favor."

Fuchsia glanced past him through the window. They were flying through cloud. "Yes, of course, Danny."

"That thing you do, you know, your precog talent, could you switch it on again?"

"I expect so," Fuchsia said. "You want to know if the plane's going to crash, don't you?"

"No. Well, yes, but . . ." Actually he wanted to know

if the plane *wasn't* going to crash, but even above the fear of flying he had another worry that was eating him alive since they'd left their own time. He looked at Fuchsia with her trusting gaze and came to a sudden decision. "I need to tell you something."

"You can tell me anything, Danny," Fuchsia said.

The plane hit some mild turbulence and rocked. Danny closed his eyes, but for once it wasn't in terror. He opened them again to look at Fuchsia. "Did you ever wonder what would happen if Cobra doesn't agree to forget his germ warfare samples?"

Fuchsia considered the question thoughtfully, then said, "No. I wondered what would happen if we couldn't find him, but I never wondered that."

"Suppose he doesn't? Suppose he decides he's going to send them through anyway?"

"Why would he?" Fuchsia asked. "You know what Mr. Carradine said: he's not crazy."

Danny dropped his voice. "Listen, Fuchsia, Cobra isn't involved in germ warfare yet. Would you agree not to do something you aren't doing anyway just because you were asked to by four kids who said they were *time travelers*? You'd think they were nuts, wouldn't you?"

"Why?" Fuchsia asked. "Cobra knows all about time travel—that's how he got the samples of Black Death in the first place."

"Cobra *doesn't* know all about time travel," Danny

told her urgently. "The future Cobra does, but we're looking for the young Cobra who's working for the CIA but hasn't joined Project Rainbow yet, doesn't know a thing about Montauk because it's not even built. He may or may not have heard a rumor going round the CIA that somebody, somewhere might be experimenting with time travel, and that's the most he has to go on."

Fuchsia frowned. "When you put it like that, you have to wonder if Mr. Carradine thought this whole thing through properly."

"Oh, Mr. Carradine thought it through, all right," Danny told her sourly. "Look at this. . . ." He glanced around to make sure none of the flight attendants was looking in their direction, then cautiously pulled the ring box Carradine had given him an inch or two from his pocket.

Fuchsia peered at it. "What's that?" Danny eased it out a fraction farther, and her eyes widened. She grinned mischievously. "Good heavens, Danny, this is so sudden!"

"It's not a ring," Danny said sourly. "Well, it is, but it's not an engagement ring." He flipped open the box, glanced round to make sure nobody was watching them, then leaned across to whisper in Fuchsia's ear. "It's a poison ring."

Fuchsia bent to stare into the box. "Poison?"

Danny nodded. "If you push a little catch, the

amethyst pops up and you've got poison in a cavity underneath. Cyanide. I don't want to open it, in case it spills."

"No, of course not," Fuchsia said. "Cyanide's pretty lethal, isn't it?"

"Kills you in ten seconds or something," Danny said. "Where did you get it?"

"Mr. Carradine gave it to me before we left."

"Why?"

"He wants me to kill Cobra," Danny told her miserably. He closed the ring box and slipped it back into his pocket. When he looked at Fuchsia, she was staring at him, appalled.

"Why does he want you to kill Cobra?" she demanded. "We're supposed to tell him not to send through the germ warfare samples."

"In case he won't listen. If he won't listen, Mr. Carradine wants me to poison him."

"You can't. You can't go around poisoning people." The shock on Fuchsia's face was almost comical. "I won't let you."

"I don't think I can either," Danny said.

"Then why did you bring the silly ring with you?" Fuchsia hissed.

"I don't know." Danny shook his head in despair. He turned away to look at the fog through the window, only to find they'd broken out of the cloud so that he was looking at clear sky. He turned back to Fuchsia. "He said it was one life against millions of lives. I can see that too. We have to stop those vials getting through."

"Did you agree? Did you say you would do it?"

Danny shook his head. "I told him no. I told him I wouldn't."

"Then why did you take the ring?"

"I don't know," Danny said again. "He said we needed insurance in case Cobra wouldn't cooperate. I suppose I thought he was right."

"Do you still think he was right?"

"No, but—"

"But what, Danny? This is a question of right and wrong. You can't just go around poisoning people—innocent people—whatever your justification."

"He's hardly innocent," Danny mumbled. "He's a germ warmonger." He knew there was something wrong with his logic the minute he said it.

Fuchsia pointed it out: "He isn't now. He's a young man who hasn't had anything to do with germ warfare yet. You just said so yourself."

"It's worse than that," Danny said. "Cobra is Mr. Carradine's *father*."

There was a long moment's silence as Fuchsia simply looked at him. Then she said, "This is crazy. It's probably not you, Danny; it's Mr. Carradine. But it's mad. You're

not Lucrezia Borgia. You don't go around poisoning people just to save the world. Have you told the others about
this?"

Danny shook his head. "No."

"You'll have to tell them," Fuchsia said. "This is
something that affects us all. As soon as we land and get
somewhere private, you must tell them."

Danny said, "Listen, you can see the future. I was
wondering if you could switch it on and have a look for
me, see if Cobra believes what we tell him. Or . . ." He
trailed off and put his hand up to his head as if to hide
his face.

"Or if you *murder* him?" Fuchsia asked incredulously.

"Sort of," Danny said wretchedly. "I can't. I know I
can't. But I'd still like you to look. Just in case."

"Just in case . . . ?" Fuchsia echoed. "You know I can't
see the future all the time." She was beginning to sound
angry.

"Yes, I know, but I thought you could try—"

"I didn't mean that," Fuchsia said. "Even when it
works, the future's not always there for me to see."

"But will you try?"

"Yes, I'll try, but if I see you poisoning him, we'll
have to find some way to stop it."

"Maybe seeing me poisoning him would mean we
could stop it," Danny said. He wasn't sure he believed

that, but any argument that might encourage her to look was worth using.

Fuchsia closed her eyes for a minute, then jerked her head in that weird little tic she'd done the last time. After a moment she opened her eyes again. "Can't," she said.

"What do you mean?" Danny asked.

"It won't switch on," Fuchsia said. She closed her eyes and tried again, but it was obvious that nothing was happening.

"Why won't it switch on?" Danny demanded. His earlier fear had been replaced by a feeling of desperation.

"I don't know," Fuchsia said. "Maybe it's because I'm upset that you're going around murdering people. Maybe—"

"I'm not going around murdering people! I've never murdered anybody in my life!"

"—it's because we're up in the air. Maybe it's because I've lost the ability. . . ."

"You can't have lost the ability!" Danny wailed so loudly that one of the flight attendants glanced suspiciously in his direction. "I need to know what's going to happen."

Fuchsia sniffed. "Well, you'll just have to wait. I'll try again later. After we land."

[23]

Opal, the American Embassy, Moscow, 1962

The American embassy on Ulitsa Chalkovskogo looked more like a renovated apartment building than a diplomatic residence. "I'm afraid our accommodation is a bit limited," the young man who'd met them remarked apologetically as he opened the car door. "We've been in negotiation with the Soviets for years to try to get a better place, but so far no movement." At the airport, he'd introduced himself as Harold Brooks Henderson, and now he smiled at Opal. "But Ambassador Thompson has left strict instructions that you're each to have your own quarters, so we'll do the best we can."

"Will we meet him today?" Opal asked.

"Afraid not. He sends his apologies—tied up with a trade mission. But he's asked me to act as your liaison, so if there's anything you need, just ask for me. Now, I expect you're tired after your flight, so I'll find somebody who can show you to your rooms and bring in your bags from the car." He walked across to have a word with the receptionist and came back with an envelope, which he handed to Opal. "This arrived for you from Washington in the diplomatic pouch."

After Opal was shown to her room, she waited until her luggage was delivered, then locked the door and opened the envelope. She felt a thrill of excitement as she drew out the sheet of paper. The printing looked a little rough until she realized it hadn't been printed at all. There were no such things as personal computers in 1962, so Mr. Stratford must have used an actual typewriter. She sat down on the bed and began to read. The style was terse:

I have made contact with Cobra and arranged a meeting. He will liaise with you at St. Basil's Cathedral, 1100 hours April 15. He will be at the cathedral main entrance. The cathedral is a half-hour walk from the embassy. Use the Moscow map in your pack. Do not, repeat not, request a car or tell anyone at embassy of your destination or your meeting. Show this letter to no one. Do not approach target unless he is alone. Approach target with caution. Use code words Kitay-gorod *to identify yourselves. (This is the name of a nearby subway station. If you approach wrong target it will appear that you are asking for directions.) Memorize Cobra's features from the enclosed picture, then destroy the picture and this document.*

The note was unsigned, but there was only one person it could have come from. Opal tipped up the envelope and tapped it. Four identical passport-sized black-and-white photographs dropped onto the bed. The face staring up at her was heavily bearded and fleshy, with a broad, flattened nose that might once have been broken. As she reached to pick one of the photos up, there was a light knocking on her door.

Opal slipped the pictures and note back into their envelope and pushed it under her pillow, but when she opened the bedroom door, it was only Michael. On a sudden impulse, she slid her arms around his neck and kissed him. As she drew back, she noted with satisfaction the surprise and pleasure on his face.

"What was that for?"

Opal smiled lightly. "I suppose I'm happy to see you."

Michael peered around her. "Are you alone?"

"Yes. Are you planning to kiss me back?" The letter from Mr. Stratford had made her almost giddy. They now had the information they needed to complete their mission, and for some reason she was convinced they *would* complete it. She simply could not imagine Cobra,

Mr. Carradine's father, would choose to ignore what they had to tell him.

"Actually, there's something I want to talk to you about."

Opal shrugged. "Me too. Come in." They'd been together for a couple of months now, and she still wasn't sure where his head was at. He was old-world courtesy personified, polite to a fault, and had yet to make a move on her she hadn't instigated. She knew he liked her—a girl could always tell—so it had to be a cultural thing. Sometimes she found his attitude endearing. Sometimes it drove her mad. She thought this might be one of the latter times.

He was looking around awkwardly as she closed the door, probably wondering if it was all right to be in a girl's bedroom without a chaperone. To set him at ease, she sat down on the edge of the bed and pulled the envelope from under the pillow. "From Mr. Stratford," she said. "He's come up trumps on Cobra."

But Michael was looking more awkward than ever. "I wonder if you'd mind if we talked about something else first? I think the others may be coming, and I'd really like to get this out of the way while we have a bit of privacy."

The expression on his face sobered her at once. "Yes, of course, Michael. What is it?"

He perched on the edge of a bedside chair, leaned forward earnestly, put his head in his hands. "Opal, there's something I have to tell you. I'm not sure how you're going to take this—"

There was a brisk knock on the door.

"Damn!" Michael swore.

"We'll talk later," Opal said as she stood up. If it had been any other boyfriend, she might have worried she was about to be dumped. But Michael had a track record for peculiar worries that really amounted to nothing at all. Shortly after they'd first met, he'd started to worry about an engagement his tribal elders had arranged for him when he was only five years old.

It was Fuchsia, looking serious for once, followed by Danny, who seemed . . . chastened somehow.

"Oh good, you're here already, Michael," Fuchsia said. "We all need to hear this. Tell them, Danny."

Danny pushed the door shut behind him. "Look, Fuchsia, I'm still not sure this is something we should—"

"Mr. Carradine wants him to poison Cobra," Fuchsia said.

Opal blinked. "He wants *what*?"

"That's not exactly what he said," Danny protested. "In fact, it isn't what he said at all."

"Murder him," Fuchsia said. "Cyanide slipped into his drink. Like a really creepy hit man or something.

Do you *believe* this?"

Danny held up both hands defensively. "Look, he was worried in case Cobra might not believe us. Might say he was going to send the samples no matter what. He just asked me to think about it."

Opal frowned. "Think about what? Killing him?"

"Not exactly," Danny said uneasily. "It was sort of . . . insurance. It was just a way of making sure." He sat down heavily on the bed. "Anyway, I never said I would."

She stared at him in disbelief. "You can't possibly poison somebody."

"I know."

Michael said, "Are you sure he was serious?"

Danny gave an exasperated sigh. "Of course he was serious. Mr. Carradine's not exactly a comedian."

"He gave him a special ring," Fuchsia said. "Show them the poison ring, Danny."

Danny pulled the box from his pocket with the expression of a small boy producing a copy of *Playboy*. Michael and Opal pressed forward to get a better look as he flipped it open.

"Is it real?" Opal asked. "Where's the poison?"

"It's underneath the stone," Danny said. "I don't want to open it."

"You'll have to get rid of it," Opal said firmly.

"How?" Danny asked. "You can't just drop a ring full of cyanide into the trash. The stuff smells of almonds and looks like salt. First kid who comes along might eat it."

"And actually," Michael said thoughtfully, "it might come in handy."

Opal stared at him, appalled. "You're not saying we *should* poison Cobra? What's the *matter* with you boys?"

"I don't think we should poison Cobra," Michael told her gently. "I'm as shocked as you are. But this is the Soviet Union at the height of the Cold War, and we don't know where we're going to meet up with Cobra. It could be somewhere dangerous, and a poison ring might be useful. As a protection."

This was a side of Michael Opal had never seen before. "Protection?" she echoed angrily. "So we shouldn't poison Cobra, but it's all right if we poison somebody else?"

"I didn't say that. I didn't even *think* that. But having a secret store of poison could prove useful. In extreme circumstances. Just in case. My father is a doctor and he—"

Opal's anger ratcheted up a notch. "Actually we *do* know where we can meet up with Cobra—St. Basil's Cathedral. I had a note from Mr. Stratford; I was just about to tell you." She glared at Michael. "I suppose you think we should poison a few Russians while they're praying in church?"

"Actually," Danny said, "Michael might have a point. I mean, I'm not going to poison Cobra, no matter what. Or anybody else, ever. But if we *did* get into a tight spot, being tortured or something, poison might get us out of it." He glanced at Michael for support. "The Nazis used cyanide to kill themselves when they were captured after the war. Mr. Carradine even mentioned that."

"Kill ourselves?" Opal gasped. She couldn't believe what she was hearing. Danny seemed to be living in a James Bond movie.

Fuchsia said suddenly, "Why don't we just flush the poison down the loo? You won't get kids eating it then." She looked at Danny. "You can keep the ring as a souvenir."

After a long moment, Danny said, "But suppose Michael's right about us being caught and tortured? If we don't have any—"

"Just shut up, Danny," Fuchsia interrupted. "You should never have taken the ring in the first place, and I'm really cross that you did." She turned very deliberately to Opal. "When are we supposed to meet with Cobra?"

"April fifteenth at eleven a.m."

"That's tomorrow morning, isn't it?" said Fuchsia.

Opal, Red Square, Moscow, 1962

R ed Square was gigantic. Some late snow had melted, leaving pools of slush around the edges of the cobble inlay. There were people about, but the place dwarfed them completely, giving the impression that the square itself was virtually empty. There was no traffic at all. Opal assumed motor vehicles were banned, but couldn't be sure. They had seen almost no cars on any of the streets—moving or parked—during the twenty-five minutes it had taken them to walk here. She wondered briefly if London had been as quiet as this in 1962.

"That must be the Kremlin," Michael said. He was holding a pocket guide and staring at the high red wall on the western side of the square.

Opal said nothing. She was still annoyed with him about his attitude to Danny's poison ring and still annoyed that Danny, despite his protestations, had taken it in the first place, even though the poison was now safely flushed into the Moscow sewers. But Michael was probably right: the complex of buildings beyond the wall almost certainly made up the Kremlin. She'd read somewhere that it had been the fortress of the Russian czars at one time. Now it housed Russia's Communist rulers.

Opal's gaze slid northward, attracted by the movement of a single uniformed soldier marching slowly, almost mournfully, beside a red and black step-pyramid structure set close to the wall. "Lenin's tomb," Michael told her quietly. She gave him a quick glance and a small smile. Now was not the time to draw out their quarrel. They were all on the same mission and only minutes away from meeting Cobra. This was a time to pull together. "That must be St. Basil's," she said.

She was now staring at a structure that looked as if it had sprung up out of a fairy tale. Even at this distance, it presented itself as an almost overwhelming array of swirling colors and red-brick towers. She counted six onion-shaped domes, but suspected there were more hidden to the rear of the building. The domed towers clustered around an enormous central spire. Michael flicked a page of his guide. "Yes, it is."

"Come on, gang!" Opal yelled. "That's where Cobra's waiting for us!" All four of them began to move across the vast square toward the cathedral.

There were far more people about as they approached

the building, although it didn't seem to be functioning as an open church. Whole portions of the façade—including what seemed to be the main entrance—were crisscrossed by scaffolding. Teams of workmen were swarming over them like bees.

"I think they're reroofing," Danny said. He squinted upward. "Copper sheeting, by the look of it."

"No sign of Cobra," Michael said hesitantly, peering through the scaffolding into what he could see of the gloomy entrance.

Opal glanced at her wrist, then remembered Mr. Stratford had confiscated their watches as what he called 'anachronistic artifacts'—items that had obviously no right to exist in 1962. "I think we're a little early," she said anyway.

"Might be another entrance," Danny said. "Why don't you keep an eye on this one, and I'll scout around and see if there are any others. I'll come back and get you if I spot him."

"I'll come with you," Fuchsia offered.

"I think maybe we should stick . . . together. . . ." Opal let the sentence trail: the two of them had already moved off and were walking briskly around the side of the cathedral. And in truth they were probably right: there were bound to be other entrances to the building and while this looked like the main one, the scaffolding made it difficult to tell for sure. Best to cover all options. Cobra might not wait too long if they failed to make contact in time, and their mission was far too important to allow for stupid mistakes.

"It's eleven o'clock. He should be here now," Michael said.

"How do you know the time?"

Michael slid back his sleeve to show a cheap windup wristwatch of obvious Soviet manufacture.

"Where did you get that?" Opal asked curiously.

"I borrowed it from Harold last night. I thought we would need to be able to tell the time." He caught her expression and added, "Harold Henderson from the embassy. The man who brought us from the airport."

Opal scanned the cathedral entrance again, but apart from the workmen, there seemed to be no one about. She began to feel faintly uneasy.

"What happens if he doesn't turn up?" Michael asked, putting her own fears into words.

"I don't know," Opal said. "I suppose we try to get in touch with Mr. Stratford and see if he can set up another meeting."

"I hope it doesn't come to that," Michael told her. "I'm not sure I like this country. The less time we have to spend in it, the better."

A workman in paint-splattered overalls stepped

off the scaffolding, carrying a bucket. He stood for a moment by the entrance as if catching his breath from the climb. Opal's eyes slid over him, then snapped back suddenly. "That's him!" she hissed to Michael.

Michael looked confused. "Where?"

"By the entrance—just where he agreed. That workman with the bucket. It's Cobra. I'm sure of it."

"Did you bring the photograph?" Michael whispered. He began to dig in his pocket for his own copy.

Opal slipped the photo from her pocket and glanced at it discreetly. Michael looked at his just as cautiously, then stared back at the workman. "You're right. What do we do now?" He slipped his picture back into his pocket.

"We make contact as arranged—what do you think we do?"

Michael was frowning. "Shouldn't we wait for the others?"

"No," Opal told him urgently. "They could be another fifteen minutes. They might even decide to stay at some other entrance. We can't tell how long Cobra is going to wait—he's undercover here, don't forget, and Mr. Stratford won't have told him who we are, so he must be nervous. We have to make contact now. The others can catch up. Besides, we don't need them. How many people does it take to tell him what will happen to his germ warfare samples? Come on!"

Cobra glanced suspiciously in their direction as they approached, and set the bucket down. A small clump of sightseers, all speaking Russian, got between them. Opal pushed through to discover Cobra had moved away from the scaffolding and was standing in shadow between the two small entrance pillars. Michael was separated from her now but would catch up. The important thing was to reach Cobra as quickly as possible.

He looked startled as she stepped into the entrance. "I'm Opal Harrington," she said softly. "Mr. Stratford contacted—" She remembered and changed it to, "Kitay-gorod." He looked at her blankly, and she wondered if she was pronouncing the Russian correctly. She suddenly wished she'd checked with somebody. It was the name of a railway station or something, Mr. Stratford had said in his note. She could have asked someone at random in the street, discovered quickly enough whether they understood her. But too late now. "Kitay-gorod," she repeated.

Michael caught up and stood behind her. "Kitay-gorod," he said, in what sounded to her a much more convincing accent.

"Kto ty, chert voz'mi?"

Opal glanced behind her. None of the sightseers was in earshot, but she dropped her voice to a whisper, just in case. "We don't speak Russian. But it's okay to use English—we're the ones you're waiting for. From Mr.

Stratford. I know he probably told you there were four of us, but the others have gone to look for you in case you were waiting at a different entrance."

"Do you want to go somewhere less public?" Michael put in anxiously.

Cobra was glaring at them furiously. "*Chto vy hotite, tovarishchi?*" he called out loudly. Then hissed, "Keep away from me!"

"What's the matter?" Michael asked in a bewildered voice.

Something was wrong. Cobra was actually looking frightened. Or maybe just excited. "Michael—" Opal began.

There were running footsteps behind them. "*Prebyvanie gde vy nahodites'!*" a rough voice called. "*Stoĭ ili budu strelyat'!*"

She spun round. Three thick-set men in wide-brimmed hats and identical gray raincoats were shouldering their way through the sightseers, who were scattering fearfully as birds.

"Run!" Michael gasped, and caught her by the arm.

But it was too late to run, too late to do anything. The men were upon them. Two of them seized Michael; the third grabbed Opal. She tried to jerk free, kicked out, and caught him soundly on the ankle. The man grunted, but did not release his grasp.

"Let go of us at once!" Opal shouted, no longer concerned who might hear. "We're from the American embassy!"

One of the men holding Michael actually laughed. "*Priznaniya uzhe!*" he called delightedly to his companions.

Then they were manhandling her away from the cathedral, across a stretch of cobbles that was now suddenly empty of people, and into the rear seat of a black Volga sedan. From the corner of her eye, she saw Cobra slide away into the shadows beneath the scaffolding. As one of the men climbed into the seat beside her, an errant thought occurred: cars seemed to be allowed in Red Square after all.

[25]

Danny and Fuchsia, Red Square, 1962

She appeared to have forgiven him for the business about the poison, for she'd taken his hand now so that they walked together like . . . friends? Boyfriend and girlfriend? He still couldn't decide how he felt about Fuchsia. In many ways she was as nutty as a fruitcake. But then, so was he. And he'd never met a girl before who made him smile so much, made him feel so comfortable. She managed to take everything in her stride.

Like right now, for example. Danny was still having trouble adjusting to the sheer *fantasy* of his situation. What had happened to him felt like science fiction rolled up in a superhero comic. He'd joined a top secret project, learned to leave his body, traveled in time, and was on a mission—literally—to save the world. (No pressure there, then.) Fuchsia, who was displaying even wilder talents, was with him, but did she seem worried, did she seem concerned? She was walking on Red Square in

Soviet Moscow during a terrifying era that had ended before she was born, and all she could say was . . .

"I'd love to see the inside of St. Vasily's," Fuchsia said. "That's what the Russians call St. Basil's, you know."

"How do you know that?"

"I probably read it somewhere. Either that or somebody told me. I've always retained odd bits of information. What do you think?"

"What do I think about what?" Danny asked.

"Going inside. I think we're allowed. At least the doors are open. I'll bet it's gorgeous inside."

They had passed two doors into the cathedral since they left Opal and Michael. Both had indeed seemed open, and Cobra was standing at neither. "It probably is," he told her, "but I think we should concentrate on what we're here for—finding Cobra."

"Yes, all right," Fuchsia said. Which was another thing he liked about her: she didn't need to get her own way.

They came close to circling the entire church before Fuchsia suggested, "Let's go back the same way in case he's appeared at any of the entrances we passed."

"Yes, okay," Danny said a little absently. From where they were standing now, he thought, he should be able to see Opal and Michael again, but he couldn't. He caught Fuchsia's arm. "Actually, let's not. I think it might be best to join the others." He moved forward without waiting for an answer and on that instant spotted Michael, who was walking purposefully toward the cathedral.

Events moved quickly after that. Danny and Fuchsia emerged into the main part of the square. Danny saw that Opal had made contact with Cobra: the agent was standing by the entrance of the church. Despite his disguise as a workman, Danny recognized him at once from the photo Mr. Stratford had sent. Opal was saying something to Cobra, but Danny was too far away to make out the words. Michael pushed through some strolling Russians and joined them. There was a brief conversation as a large black sedan pulled up. For some reason, Danny felt the beginnings of a chill in the pit of his stomach.

Three men in raincoats tumbled out of the car, with trouble written all over them. Danny drew in a sharp breath. Weird how, whatever country you were in, whatever year you were in, heavies always looked the same. Had to be their Neanderthal ancestry or something. One of the men shouted something in Russian, and all three began to run toward St. Basil's. No, strike that, began to run toward Opal, Michael, and Cobra. Danny almost shouted a warning, but stopped himself in time. It was too late to do his friends any good, and long experience had taught him never to draw attention to himself if he could possibly avoid it. Then the man grabbed Michael, who was closest, then Opal, who fought violently—Danny had to admire her—but it did no good: she and Michael were dragged to the waiting car. Cobra watched openmouthed for a moment, stepped into the shadow of the scaffolding, then turned and walked briskly away.

"Danny—" Fuchsia gasped.

Danny pulled her back a step into the shade of the building. "Keep quiet," he hissed. No way they could help Opal or Michael now. Their only hope was to stay out of sight, stay out of trouble, clock what was happening, and maybe be in a position to do something later. He tightened his grip on Fuchsia's arm in case she had different ideas.

The Russian civilians who'd been wandering near the church had all taken off, Danny noticed, probably as quick at spotting trouble as he was. The men manhandled Opal and Michael into the backseat of the waiting car, climbed in themselves, and slammed the door. The car's windows were as black as its paintwork. The vehicle drove away quickly across the empty square.

"What just happened?" Fuchsia whispered.

But Danny was less concerned with what had just happened than with what might be about to. He'd caught sight of a man in a hat standing directly underneath the scaffolding a short distance from the entrance on the side opposite to where Cobra had disappeared. He'd taken no part in the scuffle around Opal and Michael, but now he was looking directly at Danny and Fuchsia. Danny jerked her arm. "Let's get out of here!"

Maybe he should have moved casually, as if ambling innocently away, but all his instincts were screaming at him that if they didn't move fast, they'd be in at least as much trouble as Opal and Michael. Danny took off at top speed, dashing back around the cathedral, half dragging Fuchsia with him. Behind them, the man in the hat emerged from beneath the scaffolding and began to run too. He was smaller than the three who'd seized Opal and Michael and showed a disturbing turn of speed. Danny and Fuchsia raced across Red Square. Danny glanced behind him as their pursuer's hat fell off, but the man never hesitated. In fact he seemed to be gaining on them. Danny had a fleeting impression of a slim mustache and rimless glasses, before he turned back to redouble his efforts. "This way!" he called to Fuchsia, who'd slipped loose from his grip.

Fuchsia caught up with him, running fast and easily, as they turned onto one of the roads leading into Red Square, then turned again onto a side street. Despite his earlier show of speed, their pursuer was slowing now, and they quickly lost him in a maze of residential side streets. After a while they came to a cautious halt, listening.

They were in a narrow, empty back alley, neatly lined with refuse bins. "I think we've thrown him off," Danny said breathlessly.

"Who do you think he was?"

Danny shrugged. "Dunno. Russian Mafia?" He kept what he was really thinking to himself. Whoever had taken Opal and Michael were obviously no friends of Cobra. That was very clear from what had happened. As an undercover CIA agent, Cobra was at the sharpest end of his profession, in constant danger of his cover being blown. But the men hadn't seemed to be after Cobra himself. They'd made directly for Opal and Michael, giving Cobra the opportunity to walk away. It looked for all the world like some sort of kidnapping. Maybe it was the Russian Mafia after all. Maybe they targeted people who looked like tourists and held them for ransom. They might have overheard Opal or Michael speaking English and made an impromptu plan. Cobra could not have interfered: not only was it three against one, but he could not afford to draw attention to himself.

Hard on the heels of the whole little mystery came an even more important question: where had the men taken Opal and Michael? And what could Danny do about it? He'd twisted and turned so often while they were running, he no longer had the slightest idea where they were. Except that they were in a strange city in a strange country where they didn't know the language.

"What are we going to do?" Fuchsia asked, echoing his thought.

That was the million-dollar question. They were on a secret mission, so they could hardly walk into the nearest police station and report a kidnapping, could do nothing that would draw attention to themselves and put their mission at risk. They couldn't even ask the embassy for help. The most urgent thing seemed to be to try to rescue their friends, then contact Mr. Stratford and see if he could arrange another meeting with Cobra. But what could they *do* to rescue their friends? "I don't know," Danny said. "I don't even know where they've taken them."

"I do," Fuchsia said. "They've been taken to a big, rectangular, yellow brick building with a clock on top of it."

"What?"

"They've taken them to a big, rectan—"

"How do you know that?" Danny interrupted her. Then he realized. "Oh."

She smiled delightedly. "I think I'm getting the hang of it, Danny."

Danny frowned. "Are you sure about this?"

"Yes, absolutely."

Danny was experiencing a rising excitement. "Where

was it? Did you see a street name or anything?"

But Fuchsia shook her head. "No, just the big yellow brick building."

"What about a sign on the building itself?"

"Nothing. At least I didn't see anything. I mean, there were no obvious signs like 'Harrods' or 'Royal Liver Insurance.' Although it did look a bit like an insurance company, now I come to think of it."

"Like offices?"

"Yes, like a big office building."

"Was this, like, hidden away somewhere? In the country? Were there armed guards and stuff?"

Fuchsia shook her head again. "No, it's in a city square. Not as big as Red Square. No guards or anything like that. There were cars outside, and people just walked in and out. Like ordinary offices."

Danny put a thoughtful arm around her shoulder, and they began to walk out of the alley. Why would the Mafia take Opal and Michael to an ordinary office building? A public place with people walking in and out. Why would criminals expose themselves openly like that? For Danny it was getting more bizarre the more he tried to think it through. An idea occurred to him. "Could you track the route the car took on a map?"

Fuchsia stopped walking. "I don't know, but it's

worth a try. Do you have your Moscow map? I didn't bring mine."

Danny pulled Mr. Stratford's pack from his pocket and extracted the map. Fuchsia stared at it for a long time without speaking. Eventually she said, "Lubyanka Square. Not too far from St. Basil's, really. I think it's a big yellow building in Lubyanka Square."

"Okay," Danny murmured, "let's see if there's anything about it in the book of words." He pulled out the little guidebook Stratford had included and flicked through its listings. He wasn't really expecting to find Lubyanka, but there it was. He skimmed through the list of important facts about the square and felt himself go chill. "Are you sure? Are you sure it was Lubyanka?"

"No, I'm not," Fuchsia said. "But couldn't we go there and find out? I mean, the building will either be there or it won't."

Danny thought for a moment, then decided not to worry her until he was absolutely sure. "Good idea," he muttered.

It took them some time to find their bearings after they left the alley. Moscow street names were posted only in Cyrillic, which didn't tally with their map and meant as little to them as Egyptian hieroglyphs. They tried twice asking directions in English, but received only blank, suspicious looks. Eventually they found their way to the river, and a distinctive church enabled them to locate exactly where they were. Another three-quarters of an hour and they were in Lubyanka Square. It was dominated by a huge, rectangular yellow brick structure that might have been a massive office building. It even had the clock on its façade that Fuchsia had mentioned.

"That's the building I saw," Fuchsia said quietly. "What do we do now? Go in and ask for our friends?"

Danny shook his head soberly. "I don't think so, Fuchsia. That's secret-police territory. Your yellow building is the Moscow headquarters of the KGB."

[26]

Opal, KGB Headquarters, Lubyanka Square, Moscow, 1962

Opal was afraid. The men had separated her from Michael and bundled her unceremoniously into a room furnished only with an ancient desk, two chairs, and a wooden filing cabinet. The single window was shuttered, padlocked, and lacking curtains. There was linoleum on the floor, stained brown in places, worn in others. Above her head, the room was lit by a cold neon tube. When she tried the door after the men left, she discovered—not altogether to her surprise—that it was locked.

She stood for a moment, wondering what to do. The men had handled her roughly—she was bruised on her left arm—but given no indication of who they were or what they wanted from her. She had no idea where she was, why she was here, or what was going to happen to her.

She walked over to the filing cabinet and tried each of the four drawers in turn. All of them were locked. She moved behind the desk and tried its drawers, but they were locked too. The chair behind the desk was worn old leather, but more comfortable than the straight-backed wooden chair in front, and she sat down in it heavily to gather her thoughts.

"*Nyet!*" screamed a raucous voice out of the air.

Opal jumped to her feet, her heart pounding. She looked around fearfully, but could see nothing of the hidden speaker. Or the hidden camera, for it was now obvious her every move was being watched. Where *was* this place? She walked to the other side of the desk and stared at the wooden chair, wondering if she would be allowed to sit on it. But for the moment she decided not to try. She returned to the door and tried it again. It was still locked. She stood staring at the wall. It was painted a dull, uniform brown, chipped and scratched in places. She strained her ears to listen, but there were no sounds beyond the door or anywhere outside the room.

After a long while she returned to the wooden chair and placed a tentative hand on its back. She had grown tired of standing, but she was still afraid to sit down in case the voice shouted at her again. She hesitated.

There was a rattle behind her, the sound of a key in the lock. As she turned, the door opened to admit a thick-set man in his forties, wearing an ill-fitting suit. He nodded at her briefly, locked the door again, then walked behind the desk to sit in the worn leather chair. No hidden voice screamed at him. "Please take a seat, Miss Harrington," he said in flawless English, with a distinct Russian accent. "I am sorry to have kept you waiting."

He knew her name! He watched as she sat down on the edge of the wooden chair, grateful to relieve the ache in her legs, but still wary. She said nothing. Some instinct warned her to wait. It was disturbing that he knew her name. It was particularly disturbing that she had no idea how: she had not been searched, questioned, or asked for identification before they shoved her in here.

"Let me introduce myself," he said pleasantly. "My name is Menshikov. And you, I believe, are Miss Opal Harrington, a young lady who has come a long way to visit us in the Soviet Union?"

Opal took a deep breath. Part of her Shadow Project training was designed to help her stand up under interrogation (although everyone had insisted she would never need it), and a prime rule was to find out as much as possible from your interrogators before answering any questions. Starting with who they were. "Mr. Menshikov," she said firmly, "I demand to know where I am and why I have been forcibly abducted and brought here against my will."

"Actually, it's *Colonel* Menshikov, Miss Harrington.

They called me in on my day off, so I am not wearing my uniform." He held up a hand in mock protest. "I know, you are thinking this man has not the bearing of a military colonel, and I suspect you are right. But I am a colonel in the KGB—that is the *Komitet gosudarstvennoi bezopasnosti*, which is our country's national security organization—and here there are perhaps more opportunities for promotion if one does not look the part." He smiled at her, showing less than perfect teeth.

Opal felt herself go cold. Colonel Menshikov had no need to explain what *KGB* stood for: she'd seen enough spy movies to know exactly. And what it stood for at the height of the Cold War was terrifying. For now, the colonel was obviously playing with her, and not very subtly. The soft approach to find out how naive she was could be followed at any time by stronger measures. But the real mystery was why she was here. How did the KGB know her name? Why were they interested in her at all? An even more disturbing thought occurred. Although she never felt like one, her work with the Shadow Project made her a spy. Spies were tortured and shot in the Soviet Union.

Except that she'd never spied on the Soviet Union. The Soviet Union no longer existed in her time.

Abruptly, Opal decided to play along with Menshikov's ingratiating approach for as long as it lasted.

She desperately needed to know what had happened to bring her into this room. Only then would it be possible to find a way out of it. She forced her body to relax and even managed a small smile. "I can't begin to imagine why the KGB would be interested in me."

Menshikov stood up, pulled a bunch of keys from his pocket, and used one to unlock the top drawer of the filing cabinet. He extracted a manila folder, which he threw onto the desk as he sat down again. "Your file," he said conversationally. "Slim at the moment, but perhaps with your cooperation we can flesh it out a little."

"You have a *file* on me?" Opal failed entirely to keep the shock from her voice. "Where *is* this place?"

"You asked before. I thought you might have guessed by now. This is KGB headquarters. Part of the building is administration offices, part is a prison, part consists of interrogation rooms like this one—where, I hope, we will not have to delay you for long." He took a newly sharpened pencil from the breast pocket of his jacket and used it to flick up one corner of the folder. Inside she had the briefest glimpse of what looked like a single sheet of paper. Then he let the corner drop. "I have only a few questions for you, but before we get to them, let me tell you some things that will, perhaps, reassure you." The smile again, to every appearance completely genuine. "Would I be correct in assuming that my mention of the KGB has left you a little . . . shall we say, apprehensive?"

Opal forced herself to smile back, although she doubted her attempt was as convincing as his own. "Perhaps just a little."

Menshikov sat up and said briskly, "I'm afraid, as an organization, we have not been very skilled in"—he hesitated for the first time, suddenly frowning—"public relatives? Do you say 'public relatives'?"

"Public relations," Opal corrected him.

"Ah, yes, public *relations*. Forgive me: my English is very poor. As a result, there have been many misconceptions about the activities of the KGB. You will no doubt have heard that we torture prisoners, is this not so?"

It was Opal's turn to hesitate, but only for a moment. If she was to get anywhere, she had to give the impression of total honesty. "Yes."

"Then let me assure you," said Menshikov expansively, "this is not the case. KGB officers are expressly forbidden by our founding legislation to cause any physical harm to those in our custody, for whatever reason they are under investigation."

Opal's instinct was to let him talk, but he looked at her now without speaking further. With a mild sensation of panic, she heard herself ask, "What about *mental* torture?"

To her surprise, he actually laughed. "Ah, the deprivation of sleep, the loud music played endlessly through speakers, the humiliation through the removal of clothes, the forced stress positions . . . you have heard of all these things, no doubt?"

She had. "Not true?" she asked.

"Not true," Menshikov echoed. "We rely almost entirely on the willing cooperation of those we need to question."

"So if I wanted to get up and leave now, you would do nothing to stop me?"

"Oh come, Miss Harrington, you toy with me. You know there are questions I must ask you. You are obviously a sensible young woman, so it is my hope and expectation that you will cooperate with me. I fear that unless you choose to give me satisfactory answers, I am forced to detain you here until you do—that is my job. I am simply telling you that you should have no fear of torture, physical or mental, during your stay here." The easy smile came again. "Unless you count the food, of course, which I'm afraid is quite dreadful."

"But nourishing," Opal suggested ironically.

"Indeed," he said, a little blankly. He drew the file toward him and flicked it open. Then he took a thick-barreled fountain pen from his breast pocket, unscrewed the top, and set it down beside the pencil by the folder. "Now, Miss Harrington, tell me all you know about psychotronics and time travel."

[27]

Michael, KGB Headquarters
Basement, 1962

It was cold. Michael's breath plumed in time to the rise and fall of his chest. His arms were shackled at the wrists and pulled above his head by a slack chain attached to a pulley on the ceiling. His ankles were also shackled, in this case to an iron bar that left his feet spread about a yard apart. The bar was, in turn, chained to fittings sunk into a concrete block beneath him. There was nothing painful about the shackles themselves—all four felt, if anything, a little loose—but the wrist chain meant he was unable to sit or even squat, while the bar prevented his taking so much as a single step across the room. He could bend, he could turn, but these were the only movements permitted.

His arms hurt from being held up at an unnatural angle. His legs hurt even more.

The cell was somewhere in the basement of the building where the three men had brought Opal and himself.

It was windowless and lit only by a single dim bulb hanging from a length of electrical cord in the middle of the ceiling. The walls were whitewashed, with a splattering of curious brown stains. The floor was of worn stone flags. There was only one item of furniture, an old wooden chair.

Michael bent his knees to take some of the strain from his legs. Although he could not bend them much, it helped a little, but only for a moment. The problem was, bending his legs left him hanging from the chain that held his wrists, so that his arms immediately began to spasm and his shoulder sockets felt as if they were on fire. He endured it for as long as he could, then straightened his knees. His legs began to ache again.

Turning round on his own axis helped a little too. He could manage that fairly easily since the ankle bar was fixed in such a way as to allow a full 360-degree rotation. There was just enough chain to permit him to shuffle his feet. With a little concentration he could use the movement to turn slowly so that he faced each blank wall in turn. In one of them there was a steel-clad door with a sliding hatch at head height. Michael knew this had to be an observation hatch, although it had remained closed since he became aware of it. Michael even knew where he was, or thought he did. He was in a subterranean cell of the Lubyanka Prison, which formed part of KGB headquarters.

The classrooms of Eton College seemed very far away.

Despite his pain, he came close to a smile. It was in a history lesson at Eton that he'd learned about the KGB and their Lubyanka Prison. An old Soviet joke had stuck in his mind:

Why has KGB headquarters got the best view in the whole of Moscow?
Because from the basement you can see Siberia.

Siberia was where the Soviets kept their prison camps, the dreaded gulags, where dissident political prisoners spent brutal years of hard labor in subzero temperatures. Those who survived the Lubyanka itself, that was. The Lubyanka was where suspects were questioned, sometimes with such ferocity that they died.

Michael stopped his circle. The result was always the same. He could change position slightly, but ultimately it made no difference. He could ease one ache a little, but only at the expense of starting another. There was no easement, no letup. The pains had crept into his back and chest, and while no single pain was unbearable in itself, the combination of aches never stopped. There was a term for what was happening to him, and it diverted him to try to remember it. Eventually he did. He was in a 'stress position.' If you had to endure a stress position long enough, you would tell your captors anything.

He had no idea how long he had hung in this stress position. He thought it must be at least an hour, although it might well have been longer. It certainly felt longer. Time stretched endlessly when your body was filled with pain. He wished he had one of the Shadow Project's psychotronic helmets. With that he could leave his body and its ills. Without it, he was trapped.

Facing the cell door, Michael slumped forward and hung by his arms to ease the fire that had started in his calves and thighs. He set his mind to solving the mystery of why he was here, partly to take his mind off the pain, partly because it was important to work out some sort of strategy before his captors returned.

Why had the KGB shown this sudden interest in four young visitors to the American embassy? They were, admittedly, secret agents of a sort as members of the Shadow Project, but that was years in the future, with no possibility of the KGB discovering it. No documentation existed anywhere. There was no reason for the Soviet authorities to see them as anything more than innocent visitors. So why had they been taken? The Russians must have had some reason, and a pressing one.

He still needed to work out what that reason was. He

reviewed the situation. One thing stood out. They had been seized as they made contact with Cobra. This was surely not a coincidence. Cobra was a CIA agent, working undercover on heaven-knew-what sort of mission. If Cobra's cover had somehow been blown, he and Opal might have been arrested as part of the fallout, innocent (or not-so-innocent) bystanders who just happened to be in the wrong place at the wrong time.

The only problem with that theory was that Cobra himself had not been arrested. At least, Michael didn't think he had. But it was possible to imagine the KGB might have a reason for that. For example, Michael could envision a scenario in which he and Opal were arrested in order to panic Cobra into revealing himself, or running for safety and hence revealing others who might be involved in his operation. There were so many—

Michael jerked upright and swallowed desperately to clear a dry throat. There was a key inserting into the lock of his cell door.

The man who entered smelled of cheap cologne and hair cream. Michael mistrusted him at once. He stared at Michael almost blankly for a moment, then pushed the door so that it closed slowly with a soft click. He did not relock it, but instead dropped the key into the side pocket of his jacket.

"Michael Potolo," he said in English. "Is it true you

are a prince in your own country? Should I address you as *Prince* Michael? *Et peut-être vous préférez que nous parlions en français?*"

Name, title—and since he knew Michael's native language, almost certainly he knew his country of origin. The shock was almost palpable, but Michael fought hard not to let it show. "In English," he said, and was surprised how difficult it was to speak. His voice emerged as a dry croak.

"As you wish. I am fluent in either tongue. Allow me to introduce myself. I am Colonel Menshikov of the KGB. You have heard of the KGB, no doubt?"

There was something in the angle of his arms and the cramping of his chest muscles that made it literally painful to speak, as if something was jabbing into his lungs. But it was important to show no weakness. Michael murmured, "Yes."

Menshikov dragged the wooden chair across the floor until it was hardly more than a foot or so away from Michael, then sat down. He reached into his breast pocket, pulled out a slim silver cigarette case, and extracted a black, gold-tipped cigarette. "May I offer you a cigarette?"

"No." Michael shook his head and immediately regretted it as a new pain flowed into his neck.

"A pity." Menshikov placed the cigarette slowly in his

mouth, lit it with a flip-top lighter, and drew smoke deep into his lungs. He removed the cigarette and stared at it fondly between his fingers.

"Ah well," said Menshikov briskly, "I must not keep you waiting. First, I must apologize for your degree of discomfort. Should you elect to answer a few questions, it will be relieved at once. Do you understand?"

Michael nodded his head, unwilling to risk the pain of speaking more than he had to. Despite the cold, he felt a single bead of sweat begin to trickle down his forehead.

Menshikov tilted his head to one side and stared at him shrewdly. "Is it painful for you to speak?" he asked sharply.

Michael nodded again.

"An error of judgment on the part of my subordinates. I wish to encourage you to talk, not make it difficult." He stood up and quickly made an adjustment to the length of the chain holding Michael's arms. "A little easier?"

Michael felt the relief at once. "Yes."

"Ah, good." Menshikov sat down again. He smiled warmly at Michael. "I require a few words from you on certain topics, just a few words to show willingness; then you can be released and your belongings returned to you, and we may continue our conversation in a more civilized manner." The smile disappeared abruptly. "If, however, you refuse to speak, I fear your current level of discomfort will be greatly increased. In fact, I shall be forced—with great reluctance—to deliver you into the hands of the Krylov twins. You have perhaps heard of the Krylov twins?"

Michael watched him, saying nothing.

Menshikov shrugged. "Perhaps they are less well known than I imagined. Grigory and Anna Krylov. I thought everyone in Moscow knew of them, even a visitor such as yourself. They are, one might say . . . specialists. But hopefully there will be no need for you to discover the extent of their talents. Or your charming companion, come to that."

Michael was instantly alert. "What do you mean?"

"Your companion Miss Harrington. I have just had the pleasure of speaking with her. I'm afraid she was not very forthcoming, so I left her to ponder on her situation while I attempt to find out if you might be a little more cooperative. If you are not, the Krylovs will visit you both. You first, since you are already prepared and since it will allow you to think on what will subsequently happen to your pretty girlfriend."

He knew Opal's name as well! And the threat behind his words was obvious. Michael licked dry lips. "What do you want to ask me?"

"First, your knowledge of psychotronics."

The fear in Michael's stomach ratcheted up another notch. Psychotronics was the technology used in the Shadow Project to stimulate the out-of-body experience. It was absolutely impossible for Menshikov to have heard about it unless he knew all about the Shadow Project as well. And he couldn't know about the Shadow Project, which had not even been formed yet, would not be formed for decades. Michael's mind whirled, then a sudden memory emerged. In his foundation briefing at the Project, hadn't someone mentioned that psychotronics had originally been developed in Eastern Europe? Not Russia but . . .

Czechoslovakia! There had been a conference sometime in the sixties at which Czech scientists announced their discovery of the new energy. Czechoslovakia didn't exist as a country anymore, not in Michael's time, but when it did exist, it had been under the influence of the Soviet Union . . . and the psychotronic conference had been held in Moscow! He was sure of it.

Michael held his face studiously blank. He couldn't remember the year of the conference—he thought it might have been later than 1962—but that hardly mattered. The conference only marked the official announcement. Scientists could well have been working secretly in the field for ten years or more. So it was possible that Menshikov could have heard about psychotronics *without* knowing anything of the Shadow Project.

But why then was he asking Michael about it?

Michael decided to bluff. "Psychotronics?" he said. "What's that?"

He had half expected Menshikov to become angry, perhaps jerk the chains to cause him more violent pain, but the colonel only shrugged. "Of course not," he said. "What would a young man know of such an obscure branch of science? You are still at school, are you not?"

"Yes."

"They do not teach psychotronics at your school?"

"No."

"Of course not," Menshikov repeated. He dropped the remains of his cigarette on the floor and extinguished it with the heel of his boot. The expressionless eyes looked up at Michael again. "Let us try something else that will, perhaps, be a little easier for you. What knowledge have you of time travel?"

He knew! He knew everything! It was the only explanation. Menshikov—the Soviet KGB—knew their names, knew about the Shadow Project, knew about Montauk. But how? How could this have happened? It was utterly impossible—and because it was utterly impossible, Michael came to a decision. Somehow, Menshikov had to be bluffing, had to be pretending to know far more than he actually did. Otherwise why would he need to ask questions? And while Michael could not see what harm it would do to admit something that would only happen in the far future, he knew with absolute certainty he should not do so. At any price.

"None," he said in answer to Menshikov's question.

Once again he tensed himself in anticipation of an angry response. Once again, Menshikov merely shrugged. "I have a meeting this evening for which I must prepare, so now I shall take my leave of you. My business will keep me occupied until at least tomorrow. I regret this will mean for you an uncomfortable twenty-four hours, but if your memory has not improved by this time tomorrow, then I fear you will experience additional discomfort still." He stared thoughtfully up at the ceiling. "On my return I shall introduce you to the Krylov twins."

Danny and Fuchsia, the American
Embassy, Moscow, 1962

What are we going to do?" Fuchsia asked.

"Dunno," Danny muttered sourly. He'd been racking his brain on just that question during the whole long walk from Lubyanka Square. They were back in the American embassy now, in Fuchsia's quarters, which, for some reason, were a bit larger than Danny's and sported two armchairs. Nothing had occurred to him on the walk, and no bright ideas were arriving to cheer him up now. They'd read up on Lubyanka Square in the briefing guide Mr. Stratford had given them, and it was trouble all the way. There was even a jail beneath KGB headquarters where suspects were held for questioning and often torture. Michael and Opal could not be in a more dreadful place in the whole of Russia. The worst of it was that Fuchsia was looking at him expectantly, as if he was her big, brave hero who solved all the problems. In real life, it was as much as he could do just to get by.

"We need to get help," Fuchsia said.

Danny shook his head. "That's not going to happen. Who would we go to?"

"Somebody in the embassy?"

"And tell them what? We're time travelers and the KGB have just snatched our friends?"

"Just the last bit," Fuchsia said mildly.

Danny thought about it. Eventually he shook his head again. "They'd ask questions."

"Of course they would. But we were sent over by the CIA. Wouldn't that be reason enough for them? We don't have to tell them we're time travelers or about Cobra or anything. We can just take the Fifth Amendment or whatever you do in America when you don't want to tell something."

"Yes, but we're not even sure where they are—Opal and Michael, I mean. All you saw was a vision of the building."

"It was more than that," Fuchsia cut in. "What I saw was like a sort of road into the future—I call it a time line. When I followed it, I got visions of the kidnapping and the car the men put them in and the route where it went. It stopped at KGB headquarters."

"But you didn't see them going in, did you? You never mentioned it if you did."

Fuchsia shook her head. "No, not actually going in,

but I assumed they must have. Don't you think so?"

"I don't know," Danny said honestly. "Maybe they just stopped in the square and abandoned the car, took them somewhere else in another car, or whatever, to throw off any pursuit. My problem is, I can't think of a reason why the KGB should take them at all. A criminal kidnapping makes more sense—thugs looking for a ransom. And if we tell the embassy it was the KGB and it wasn't, they're not going to believe us if we then say it was criminals." An idea struck him with the speed and force of an avalanche. He gripped Fuchsia excitedly by the shoulders. "Wait a minute—we could find out!"

"How?"

"You could do your time thing! You could see if telling them it was the KGB actually worked; if they helped us and if it did any good."

"No, I can't," Fuchsia said. "I told you before, I can only see the future once it goes solid. That part of the future will only go solid when we make our decision. Right now it's just a whole lot of misty possibilities."

"All right," Danny said. "Suppose we make a decision now to ask for help at the embassy. Why don't we decide that now, and then you have a look and see where the time line leads, and if it doesn't lead to Michael and Opal getting free, then we don't do it."

"That's not a decision, is it? That's only a decision

if things work out right, so we don't have a solid future yet."

"Let's try it anyway," Danny said.

"Okay," Fuchsia said.

She lay down on the bed and closed her eyes. Danny watched her carefully. For a long time she just lay there, then her head made the peculiar jerking motion. "Can you see it?' he asked impatiently, but she didn't answer. After a while she opened her eyes.

"It didn't work."

"But you were in the zone!" Danny protested. "I saw you."

"Yes, but there's no solid future: just misty possibilities."

Danny still wouldn't let it go. "Did you look to see if they do manage to get out at all? I mean, maybe not because of us, but for any reason sometime in the future? Did you look at the misty possibilities?"

"I looked at some of them. Sometimes they do get away, sometimes they don't." She hesitated. "Sometimes they're dead," she added quietly.

"What's that mean?" Danny demanded almost desperately. "You're not making any sense."

Fuchsia swung her feet off the bed. "That's because *it* doesn't make any sense. Or maybe you're right—maybe it's just me. I'm really new to this, Danny. I couldn't do it at all before we traveled in time."

Danny sat down on the bed beside her and nodded. He had the feeling that he might have been a little hard on her. "I know."

There was a long, thoughtful silence. Eventually Fuchsia said, "I wish we had one of the helmets."

Danny lay down on his back on the bed and closed his eyes. "What helmets?"

"Those things they have in the Shadow Project. You could put it on and search KGB headquarters in your astral body. That's what you do, isn't it? You could search to see if they're still there, and it might give us some idea how to get them out. Or at least let us know they're still all right."

There was another lengthy silence. This time it was Danny who broke it. "I can do it without one."

Fuchsia twisted to look at him. "What did you say?"

Danny pushed himself reluctantly upright. "After I did my first helmet projection and got used to being out of my body, I discovered I could do it without the helmet. It was a bit tricky, but I was sort of desperate because they'd locked me up at the time."

"Do you think you might be able to do it again?"

"Can't hurt to try. And if we know for sure they're with the KGB, then we can definitely go to the embassy for help."

"What do you do?"

"Lie down, I think," Danny said. "Unless you'd rather I tried it from one of the armchairs."

"No," Fuchsia told him, "you lie down on my bed. I'll sit in the armchair and watch you."

"I don't want you to talk to me—that's too distracting."

"All right."

"And you mustn't touch me, because that can jerk me back in."

Fuchsia grinned at him. "I'll try to resist the temptation."

"Should we do it now?" Danny asked hesitantly.

"Yes, of course," Fuchsia told him. "The sooner the better. I'll watch over you and wait patiently and not even dream of touching you, and you see what you can find out; and then when you come back, I'll see if anything you've found out has generated a time line to a solid future."

"I'll take my shoes off," Danny said. "So I don't mess up your bed." He was aware he was stalling. He was afraid he might not be able to find their friends. When she didn't reply, he added, "Yes, well, all right, let's get started." He kicked off his shoes without undoing the laces and stretched out on his back on the bed. He saw Fuchsia sit in the armchair just before he closed his eyes.

There were probably better ways of doing it, but Danny didn't know them. And he wasn't even sure that this way was going to work. The fact that he'd managed it before was no guarantee he'd be able to do it again. But he had to try.

He thought of Fran, the Shadow Project operative who'd trained him.

During his training, just before she . . . died, she'd set up something called a standing wave of sound, which had made him feel as if his insides were falling out. He concentrated on that feeling now, trying to re-create it, trying hard not to think of what else had happened after she'd switched on the standing wave. But the problem was, his mind kept going from the standing wave to the demon that had ripped Fran's throat out. He knew that he would forever link that demon with leaving his body, that a part of him still expected it to appear again. It was completely illogical—the demon was dead; he'd killed it himself—but he could not shake the worry, and the worry distracted him from what he should be doing.

Danny called on all his powers of concentration and focused on the sick sensation produced by the standing wave. Eventually he found it, faintly at first, no more than the sort of queasy feeling you get from eating one hotdog too many. But now he felt it in his stomach, not just as a memory. And as he concentrated, he could feel it growing stronger.

With the queasiness came an associated memory, and he began to feel shaky. Then the shake became a vibration, and he knew at once he was going to succeed. He took a deep breath, sank back somewhere inside his head, and let it happen. The vibration became more intense, then actively violent, almost unbearable, until he thought he was going to shake to pieces. But then, without warning, it stopped.

Danny lay quite still, welcoming the sudden peace. He did not try to move, because he knew from experience he would not be able to. The paralysis had been terrifying the first time it happened. Now he kept telling himself it would soon wear off; all he had to do was wait for the bats.

They weren't bats, of course. He wasn't even sure they were living creatures. At the Project they'd been named Guardians, or Threshold Guardians, since they seemed to appear just as you were about to leave your body. They were shapes and they flew around your head and they looked a bit like bats. Danny was the only Project operative who could see them around other agents as well as himself.

It seemed to take a very long time—probably just because he was feeling impatient—but the bats finally appeared, flitting around his head, perfectly visible despite the fact he had his eyes closed. Then, abruptly, they disappeared and he could move again. He opened his eyes and stretched. His arms reached above his head, penetrated the headboard and the wall beyond. He drew them back and swung his feet off the bed onto the floor. As he sat up, he could see Fuchsia seated in the armchair, unaware of what he was doing.

Danny glanced back at his physical body, still lying on the bed, eyes closed as if asleep. Then he turned and walked quickly through the wall on his way out of the embassy building.

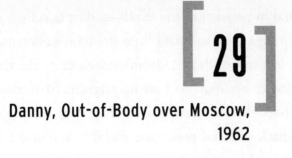

[29]

Danny, Out-of-Body over Moscow, 1962

Danny flew. The feeling of exhilaration was so great that he had made several preliminary circles about the building before he realized he had no idea how to get back to Lubyanka Square. The city below him was a maze of confusing streets, avenues, boulevards, and squares, crisscrossed by major arteries that looked completely unfamiliar. He tried to re-create his memory of the walk back to the embassy on the territory below and failed. The viewpoints were just too different.

He felt a swelling of frustration. Often, in the astral body, it was possible to reach a location just by thinking of it: "Gross movement follows thought" was a training maxim at the Project. But for that to work, one of two conditions had to be in place. Either your target was in sight, however distantly, or you were so familiar with it that you could visualize it clearly and in detail. He had only seen KGB headquarters once, and while he had a general impression in his mind—yellow building, clock set up high—he had paid little attention to details, and even less to details of Lubyanka Square. At the time it had never occurred to him he might need to find his way back there without a street map. And the one great drawback of astral projection was that you could bring nothing with you.

Hazy though it was, he called up a picture of the building as best he remembered it, closed his eyes, and willed himself to go there. Even before he opened them again, he knew he had not succeeded. He tried again, eyes open this time. When gross movement really did follow thought, the results were instantaneous. One clock tick you were *here,* the next you were *there.* But however hard he tried to visualize now, he remained stubbornly *here.*

Danny's frustration grew into a simmering anger, directed mainly at himself. The problem was, he had not thought of using his out-of-body ability to help his friends until Fuchsia brought it up. It was infuriating. If the idea had occurred to him earlier, while he was in Lubyanka Square, he could have studied the KGB building more carefully, ensured he could get back there any time he pleased. But he hadn't and now he was stuck with the consequences.

He thought briefly of returning to his physical body, collecting a map, and walking back to the target building, but dismissed the idea at once. He would waste far too much time getting there and back when only God knew what dangers Opal and Michael were facing. There had to be a faster way. He hovered three hundred feet above the ground, staring out across the cityscape, and forced himself to think.

It occurred to him abruptly that he was being stupid. He was in the air now. He didn't have to follow streets the way he did while he was on the ground. In the air, you thought in terms of general directions, looked for landmarks, then used them to orient yourself. In the air, you could see broad swaths of the city, whereas on the ground you could only see the road ahead. As a general direction, he was sure Lubyanka Square lay somewhere to the east of the embassy he'd just left. Possibly not due east, but . . .

Another thought occurred to him. What *did* lie due east of the embassy was Red Square, and Lubyanka was hardly more than half a mile away from there. If he could find his way to Red Square, he should be able to locate Lubyanka fairly easily. And he could surely find Red Square—it was the biggest square in Moscow.

Danny flew upward until the city turned into a panoramic network. He spotted the Moskva River at once, and while it was not a landmark he could use directly, it did help him maintain a sense of direction. He dropped his altitude again and began to fly carefully east, keeping the river in sight.

It was difficult to judge speed while out of the body. Travel by the gross-movement-follows-thought principle was instantaneous as far as anybody in the Project could judge. Cruising, as most operatives referred to what he was doing now, could vary greatly from a leisurely bird-like swoop to something more resembling a rocket or a jet plane. But there was no air against the face, no rushing in the ears, so only the apparent movement of the ground below gave him much of a clue to his momentum. All the same, he seemed to have been flying fast and long with no sign of Red Square.

He racked his brain for any other memory of the city and, after a moment, one laboriously emerged. Red Square lay just north of the river: he remembered that much from his earlier glances at the map. At this height, all he had to do was watch what bordered the river to the north and he was bound to see Red Square. Unless he'd already passed it, of course. But just as the thought occurred, he spotted it—not Red Square itself, but the vivid towers of St. Basil's Cathedral, where his friends had been kidnapped.

Danny dropped lower in order to make sure—there seemed to be quite a few colorful churches and cathedrals scattered throughout Moscow—but it was St. Basil's, all right. He could see the Kremlin across the square and, as he lost height, could even pick up the distinctive outline of Lenin's tomb. Now it was only a question of finding Lubyanka Square.

He turned north and took a slow, serpentine flight path, fanning alternately east and west. Lubyanka might be north of Red Square, but not directly north, and this was a way of making sure he did not miss it. All the same, he seemed to have traveled well over half a mile without seeing anything he recognized. He was beginning to wonder about returning to Red Square and trying a broader sweep when a flash of yellow caught his eye. Excitedly, Danny swooped toward it. As he came closer, his excitement turned to triumph. He could see the façade now, with its yellow brickwork. He could see the clock set into the building's topmost floor.

Danny landed delicately as a butterfly and stood staring up at KGB headquarters.

It was nearing sunset, a time when offices would shut for the evening, but there was no sign of this place closing. Lights were coming on behind many of the windows, and people still entered and left by the main doors. As before, there were few cars on the street, but there were large numbers of people in the square. And this time he noticed something about them that had not struck him before: those who didn't enter the building walked past it hurriedly, their eyes firmly downcast, like people hoping they would not be noticed. It was as if the building frightened them.

A pedestrian walked through him, headed for the main doors. Danny made a snap decision and walked quickly after her. The studded door closed again in his face, but he walked straight through it into a narrow, featureless hallway guarded by a dour receptionist seated behind an old-fashioned wooden desk with score marks across its surface. The visitor ignored her, but produced an ID card for the uniformed guard at the entrance to the broad foyer beyond—Danny thought she must be a KGB employee, somebody's secretary perhaps, who knew the workings of the building inside out and was a familiar face to casual security.

Danny moved toward the guard as the woman he'd been following disappeared into the deeper reaches of the building. The man looked through him blankly. The foyer beyond was grandiose, with pink marble pillars, an inlaid marble checkerboard floor, and several white-painted doors leading off. On his right was a broad stone staircase leading to the upper stories. As he glanced up, he could see a life-size statue of some Russian dignitary waiting on the first landing.

Where to go? KGB headquarters was five stories high and quite gigantic. He could imagine the interior as a warren of offices and corridors. Opal and Michael could be anywhere, and even though he could go where he liked without challenge, it might take him hours to find them. Which was a good reason to get started, except that he couldn't make up his mind *where* to start.

Danny stood beside the guard and looked around, trying to decide. If Opal and Michael had been seized by the KGB (and he could think of no other explanation for their being taken here), then they were surely under suspicion of something. It was hard to think what—nobody in 1962 could possibly know anything about their mission—but the Soviets were clearly paranoid, so simply staying in the American embassy might be enough to draw attention to them. For all he knew, grabbing foreigners off the street might even have been standard practice during the Cold War. But what would be the next logical step after that?

Being out of his body allowed him to move about like a ghost, flying through the air and passing through doors or walls, but he certainly didn't feel like a ghost. He felt exactly as if he was still in his physical body. Danny experienced a chill as a thought occurred to him. Beneath KGB headquarters was Lubyanka Prison, where, their briefing guide said, suspects were held and tortured. Was that where he should start looking for Opal and Michael? He pushed the thought aside. He needed to get this whole thing into perspective. Opal and Michael were obviously being questioned somewhere, but there was no way they would warrant a jail cell or torture. Far more likely they would be in a perfectly civilized office somewhere, chatting over a cup of tea or whatever it was Russians drank, before being sent back to the embassy once the KGB was satisfied they weren't about to overthrow the government. Maybe he and Fuchsia were panicking unnecessarily. Maybe it would all work itself out inside an hour or two.

And maybe he was about to get a knighthood for services rendered, Danny thought cynically. He'd had his own run-ins with the law, and even in a best-case scenario he knew that if they'd been held this long, their chances of release before tomorrow were slim. And every hour that went by was one more hour when they weren't talking to Cobra, weren't even starting to sort out the mess around the whole Cobra business. All the same, he still thought the basement prison was unlikely. He decided to start on the fifth floor, fly quickly through every office he could find, then drop down a floor and do the same thing if he hadn't found Opal and Michael, repeating the process until he *did* find them.

But the little voice in Danny's head wouldn't leave him alone. What if they weren't in any of the five floors he was going to explore? What if he didn't find them?

Then I'll go down to the basement—all right? he told the little voice savagely. Sometimes Danny knew things about himself he'd rather not have known, and at the moment he knew he didn't want to visit Lubyanka Prison. You could still smell blood when you were in your second body.

Using the stairwell as his guide, Danny floated quickly upward to the topmost floor.

He found Opal almost at once. He entered a small room with a single curtained window, and his eye was drawn immediately to a combination desk and seat, like the sort of thing you sat in at elementary school, set against one wall. Beside it was an open lavatory bowl and a sink with only one tap. Set against the opposite wall was a bunk bed. It took him a moment to realize there was someone curled on the bed, a moment more to realize it was Opal.

Danny went directly to her. She had her face toward the wall and seemed to be asleep. Or knocked unconscious. But her breathing was deep and regular, and there was no immediate sign of any injury. . . . He walked through the bunk and turned, standing partially inside the wall, so that he could get a better look at her face. It was almost covered by one arm, but from what he could see she was all right. He moved out again, back into the room, and took another, proper, look around. It wasn't the Ritz, that was for sure. He moved to the door.

Although he couldn't try to open it—his hand would just sink helplessly into the handle—the thing was so ill-fitting that close up he could see partway through the crack between the door and the jamb. As he'd suspected, the door was locked. He could see where it was bolted across.

He wished Opal would wake up. He couldn't talk to her, of course. While she was still locked in her physical body, she couldn't see him in his astral, couldn't hear a word he might say, even if he shouted in her ear. All the same, he'd have liked to see her move around, just to be sure there were no broken bones, no limp or anything else that would suggest a beating. But Opal didn't wake up, didn't even turn in her sleep. He wanted to shake her, but that was as impossible for him now as turning the doorknob.

"Opal!" He tried anyway, shouting at the top of his lungs, just in case some hint of psychic talent caused her to pick up an echo of his voice, but she did not stir. Nothing more he could do here. His next step had to be to find Michael, who was probably somewhere nearby. Danny made a mental note about the position of the room and stepped out into a green-painted corridor with plain wooden doors every few yards. Some, he noted at once, had small metal nameplates set above head height.

He floated up to examine one more closely, but the lettering was Cyrillic and meant nothing to him.

He began to examine the other rooms and ran into difficulties immediately. Those closest to Opal's room were all offices—in one of them there was a balding man with glasses working late at a massive desk—but none contained Michael. When he returned to his earlier plan of swooping quickly through the building walls floor by floor, he soon discovered he could not keep mental track of where he'd been. Almost every room was an office, almost all were occupied, and there was a sameness about both the paintwork and the people that made one blend into another. With a sinking feeling he realized that if he was going to search this massive building properly, he needed a different approach.

For a while he tried staying in the corridor he'd found, moving from one door to another, sticking his head through the woodwork to find out what was inside, withdrawing when there was no sign of Michael, then moving to the next door. It was painfully slow, and he quickly discovered branching corridors with their own closed doors and not a single marking he could understand. To make matters worse, the KGB seemed to work twenty-four hours a day, for after an initial lull, he discovered the main corridors were often filled with people, men and women, some in uniform, some in civilian clothing, all busily going about their business. It was confusing in the extreme. It occurred to him within five minutes that he could easily have missed Michael half a dozen times.

Danny stopped to think, pressed instinctively against a corridor wall to avoid a group of women walking past. Now that he'd confirmed Opal was here, did he really need to find Michael as well? They'd both been seized by the same men, which meant Michael had to be in this building somewhere. Surely that was the only thing that mattered? Fuchsia was right when she'd said they needed help from the embassy—some sort of diplomatic approach to assure the Soviets that Opal and Michael were harmless and should be released at once. And now that he was absolutely sure their friends were being held by the KGB, they could get that help. No need to mention time lines or astral projection, of course; they could simply claim they'd seen Opal and Michael taken into the big yellow building in Lubyanka Square and let the embassy put two and two together. Let the embassy figure out why, as well. Danny certainly had no idea why the KGB had taken an interest in them. What he needed to do was get back to his physical body at once and see if they could get a meeting with the ambassador.

All the same he hesitated. Something was niggling at the back of his mind, demanding he should find out if Michael was all right. Danny closed his eyes and sank through six floors.

When he opened them again, he was in Lubyanka Prison.

[30]

Danny, Out-of-Body, Lubyanka Prison

The contrast with the upper offices was striking. Danny found himself in another corridor, this time with plain brickwork and a stone floor relieved only by a strip of plain linoleum. Here too there were doors every few yards, but unlike the wooden doors above, they were faced in metal with grilles at head height. Somewhere, distantly, someone was screaming. The noise echoed hollowly.

Unlike the bustling corridors above, this passageway was empty. Perhaps the prison officials did not work in the evenings, unlike their administration comrades. The scream came again, and Danny felt himself go chill. Perhaps *somebody* was still working. He didn't think the victim was Michael—the sound was too high-pitched. But then again, he had no idea how Michael would sound if he was . . . if he was being . . .

With huge reluctance, almost without willing it,

Danny began to move toward the sound. He floated rather than walked, passing easily, almost mindlessly, through obstructing walls and doorways (and on one occasion a short stone staircase). He had mental pictures of some hideous torture chamber, but when he reached his destination, he found himself in another passageway, almost identical to the one he'd just left. The screaming, now almost continuous, was coming from a cell a little way along. Sick to his stomach, Danny floated down the corridor and entered the cell.

There was an old man inside, seated on a wooden bench and wearing only prison trousers. There were ancient scars across his chest and arms and what looked like a burn on the index finger of his right hand. One ankle was manacled to a chain attached to the foot of his bench, but the chain looked long enough to allow him to walk anywhere inside his cell if he wanted to.

The old man looked up as Danny entered, and for a moment Danny could have sworn the prisoner had seen him. He stared at Danny fixedly for a moment, wild eyes underneath an unruly shock of gray-white hair, then began a mewling sound deep in his throat that rose in pitch and volume until it became another scream that went on and on impossibly, as if he had an infinite reserve of breath. There was no one else in the cell, no reason for the old man to be screaming.

Except memories, Danny thought.

Danny withdrew. There was nothing he could do for the prisoner, nothing he could do for anyone while he was in his astral body. Except observe and hope it took a long time to drive anyone as mad as the old man. Michael had only been here for a few hours. If Michael was here at all.

For the next three-quarters of an hour, Danny searched. It was far easier here in one way than it had been above. The prison was a great deal smaller than even a single floor of the building above, obviously no more than a converted basement. Part of it was taken up by a guardroom where two uniformed men smoked and played a listless game of cards. Part, which made Danny sick to his stomach, was devoted to a modern torture chamber, currently mercifully empty. There were also several offices (radio sets seemed to be standard equipment) and a long, narrow, cramped kitchen, which surprised him until he thought about it: even KGB prisoners had to be fed. But while there were exactly one hundred and ten cells—he counted them carefully— fewer than thirty were occupied.

None that he found was occupied by Michael.

Danny felt a surge of relief that almost made him dizzy. Many of the occupied cells housed prisoners in overalls or civilian clothes who would not have been out of place in a conventional jail. Their cells had bunks and toilet facilities, and a few were equipped with tables, chairs, and, in a handful, even bookshelves. Their occupants looked frightened, bored, miserable, as prisoners usually did, but showed no immediate signs of severe ill treatment. But in sharp contrast with these prisoners, there were others who were half-dressed, bruised, and bloody from what were clearly recent beatings. Some were shackled in uncomfortable positions. Two were actually hanging by their arms from the ceiling. It was clear the KGB was ruthless in the methods it employed. He was glad Michael had not been forced to endure them.

Danny floated upward into the ground-floor foyer of the headquarters building above. He'd more than half decided to head back to Fuchsia in the embassy, but it still niggled that even though he was fairly sure now Michael was safe and unharmed, the fact was, he hadn't been able to find him. On impulse he decided to try a few more rooms at random, and since he'd visited none at all on the ground floor, he thought he might start there.

Unlike those on the other floors, the ground-floor doors were large, paneled, and painted a glossy white. Danny passed through the nearest of them and discovered he was in a spacious, well-furnished conference room where a meeting was already taking place. The room was dominated by a large, highly polished oak table strewn with maps. Around it stood several men in army uniforms, some of whom Danny recognized from his meanderings upstairs as KGB. Beyond them, lounging in a leather armchair, was a heavily bearded man in battle fatigues. His uniform carried no insignia of rank, but he was holding a brandy glass and smoking a fat cigar, which in Danny's book meant he had to be pretty important. Near him, another armchair was occupied by a civilian in his early fifties, the only man in the place out of uniform. Between them sat a nervous, fresh-faced young man whose uniform looked brand-new.

"*¿Cuándo son enviados?*" The bearded man took a sip of his brandy and smiled broadly. His teeth were very white against the black of his beard.

The nervous young man in uniform leaned across to whisper something to the civilian, who nodded soberly, then looked at his cigar-smoking companion. "*Skoro. Yest' diplomaticheskoĭ tonkosti zavershit' v protivnom sluchae amerikantsy ne budet dovolen.*" As the young man translated, the bearded man began another slow smile, which quickly changed into a hearty laugh.

Danny lost interest. Without Russian or Spanish—it sounded like Spanish the bearded man was speaking—Danny had no idea at all what they were saying. It was obviously some sort of military meeting, but there was no reason to—

He stopped, his attention caught by the maps on the

table. One was a large sea chart with five circles drawn on it, their common center near the westernmost tip of an island that lay just south of what looked like the edge of a major landmass, but all its features were marked in Cyrillic, so they meant nothing to him. The other maps, without exception, were of the island itself. None of them was named, and he didn't recognize the long, thin, rather drooping shape. A black-and-white outline version of the island had hand-drawn boxes marking three locations: San Cristóbal, Guanajay, and, farther east, Sagua la Grande. This time the lettering was Roman, not Cyrillic, and the place names sounded Spanish. But Spain was part of a continent, not an island, so this had to be somewhere else—probably somewhere off the coast of South America.

Danny tore his eyes away from the maps. Fascinating though this meeting was, it didn't bring him any closer to finding Michael. He made a sudden decision. He'd wasted enough time already. He'd found Opal, and Michael couldn't be very far away. The important thing was to get them out. And that meant getting help from the embassy.

Danny turned away from the table and floated from the room, all the way out of the building. Then he lifted into the air and set a course back to the American embassy.

[31]

Opal, KGB Headquarters, 1962

Opal awoke with a start as the door of her room slammed back. Two uniformed men burst in, each carrying rifles.

"Vstavaĭ!" one shouted at her angrily.

She didn't understand Russian, but the meaning was clear enough. She swung her feet off the bed and stood up, silently thanking heaven she'd fallen asleep fully clothed. She doubted very much that these men would have shown much respect for her modesty. As it was, her heart was pounding with fear. Both men looked like brutes. Neither showed the least hint of Menshikov's earlier cool courtesy.

"Poĭdem s nami!" the second man shouted. Opal looked at him blankly, and he gestured with his rifle so that she had the sense he wanted her to go with them. But where were they taking her?

She tried desperately to estimate how long she'd been

asleep. It felt like a short time, but she vaguely remembered a dream that seemed to go on forever. Could it be morning already? The window of her room had padlocked shutters and a heavy curtain, so there was no way to see if it was daylight outside. Menshikov had promised to return in the morning, so perhaps these men were taking her to him.

As the confusion of sleep fell away from her mind, old fears tumbled in. Menshikov had been courteous and reassuring when her interview began, but when she claimed to know nothing of time travel or psychotronics—how had he known to ask her about either of those?—the mask had slipped a little. Not that he'd threatened her openly, but it was clear he did not believe her denials, and there were veiled hints that continued lack of cooperation might soon create problems. But what worried her far more than these hints was the fact he would tell her nothing about Michael. When she asked, he simply shrugged and claimed Michael was not his responsibility. When she pushed, he told her blankly he had "no information."

She would have given anything to know if Michael was all right.

The men used their rifles to prod her toward the door, then marched her down two corridors until they reached an elevator. The second corridor had windows on an outside wall, which allowed her to discover it was dark outside. As they waited for the elevator to arrive, she stared out across the lights of the city, trying to estimate the time. By her best guess it seemed to be the middle of the night, but it might be earlier; possibly a lot earlier. But if it wasn't almost morning, when Menshikov was returning, where were they taking her?

Her mind began to feed her stories she'd heard about the interrogation techniques used by totalitarian states. Sleep deprivation was high among them. You were allowed no sleep at all or, alternatively, permitted to sleep only a short time, then dragged awake for questioning while your resistance was at its lowest ebb. Was this what was happening to her now?

The elevator arrived with the sort of mechanical clatter she associated with a railway station. One of her guards pulled aside the old-fashioned trellised doors, and the other pushed her inside so brutally that she almost fell. They took their places on either side of her, closed the doors again, and pulled sharply on a heavy metal knob. The lift began a slow, shuddering descent.

Opal fought hard to control an almost overpowering fear. "Do either of you speak English?"

Neither guard answered, neither guard looked at her.

Opal licked dry lips. "Can you tell me where you're taking me?"

"Zatknis'!"

She didn't have to be a Russian speaker to get the sense of that one either. The man's intonation was enough. She closed her mouth and stared blankly ahead as the elevator continued to rattle slowly downward.

A crude pointer and dial on one wall marked the rate of their descent. Four of the segments were marked only with numerals: 5, 4, 3, 2. The final one—they'd started off on the fifth floor—was labeled in Cyrillic. When they reached the ground floor, the elevator cage stopped with a jerk. Through the trellised doors she could see people waiting outside. One even moved to open the outer door, but pulled back suddenly as he caught sight of the guards. The guards themselves made no move to open the doors, let alone get out. After a moment, the cage shuddered, then resumed its descent. It dropped a single floor farther before stopping again. Opal looked up at the pointer. It was centered in the final segment. They were obviously below street level. The men had taken her into some sort of basement. Opal felt her heart begin to race again and could do nothing to control it.

They emerged into a passageway with brick-lined walls and a stone-flagged floor partly covered by a strip of heavily worn linoleum. For some reason a dream she'd once had about the Spanish Inquisition came flooding back to her. The passage was absolutely featureless, but its walls exuded a smell, like a mixture of stale sweat and dried blood, that made her think of human pain. Her guards slung their rifles across their backs in a single coordinated movement, took each of her arms, and marched her down the corridor. She almost stumbled when they reached a short flight of stone steps, but regained her balance in time to make note of the fact she was now in a different sort of passageway. There were still the same unplastered walls, still the same strip of faded linoleum, but now there were cell doors every few yards. Each one had metal sheeting. Each one had an observation hatch.

Opal was moving close to panic. While she was in the office or the makeshift bedroom, she could tell herself that her situation was temporary, that she might be released at any moment. But to be thrown into a cell was another matter altogether. A cell meant you were going to be held for days, perhaps even weeks.

Perhaps forever, her mind whispered disloyally.

Opal made one more try. "Why have you brought me here?" she demanded in her most assertive tone. "Where are you taking me now?"

They continued to ignore her, not even bothering to shout at her in Russian, but it didn't really matter because she found out where she was going within minutes. One guard kept hold of her arm while the other opened a cell door using a large, old-fashioned key. She assumed this would be her home for a while, but when they pushed her through the doorway, she discovered, with a sharp intake of breath, the cell was already occupied.

The door slammed behind her.

"Michael!" Opal gasped, and ran toward him. He was slumped forward, hanging by his wrists from a chain attached to the ceiling. His ankles were shackled to a bar attached to the floor. His eyes were red and staring, his face contorted with pain.

For one hideous, savage moment, she thought he might be dead, then he took a rasping breath and murmured, "Opal."

Opal instinctively wrapped both arms around him and hoisted him upward to relieve the strain on his arms. His wrists were bleeding from beneath the shackles, and his ankles were rubbed raw. For a moment she managed to hold him, but he was a sturdy, muscular boy, and her arms quickly tired. Despite every effort, he began to slip down again. "Thank you," he whispered.

"I'm sorry." Opal felt the tears on her cheeks. She grasped him again, strained to lift him back up.

Michael straightened abruptly, taking his weight on his own legs. They trembled violently, but held him. He licked his lips, which were encrusted with blood where he had bitten them. "I'm very glad to see you," he told her in that dreadful, rasping voice.

"We have to get you out of here," Opal said desperately. "This is horrible. This is . . . unacceptable." It was a stupid word to use, but she couldn't think of another one. God alone knew how long they'd left Michael like that—maybe even since they brought him here—and the pain he must be in was beyond belief.

"Menshikov's not going to let us out of here," Michael said. "Not before morning."

"Menshikov did this to you? He told me he didn't know where you were. He told me you weren't his responsibility."

Michael's legs gave way suddenly, and the chains rattled as he slumped forward to hang from the ceiling. He caught his breath. "Menshikov lied."

Opal held him again. She couldn't support his weight for long, but even a small easement of his pain had to be a help. He must have guessed what she was thinking, for he said, "It's not as bad as it looks. My legs don't hurt anymore: they've gone numb. But they won't hold me up very long, so there's a bit of strain on my arms. My shoulders are the worst."

"Your wrists are bleeding."

"Are they? I can't see. I thought they felt grazed."

He was so *brave*! She felt a surge of almost overwhelming affection for him, mixed with a white-hot rage against Menshikov. How *dare* he do something like this? If she'd had it in her power at that precise instant, she would have killed him! She reined in the anger. An emotional response wasn't going to do any good in these circumstances. What she needed was to think logically, try to figure out what was going on, make a plan to get them both out of here. She took a deep breath to steady herself. "Did Menshikov say what he planned to do with you?" There must be something planned. Torture was always applied for a reason.

"He wants information on time travel and psycho-tronics."

"He asked me about that too." She wondered suddenly why Menshikov hadn't tortured her as well. She had refused to talk, just like Michael. "I didn't tell him anything."

Michael whispered quickly, "I think there are hidden microphones in these cells."

Opal stopped short. "You know," she added casually, "I don't even know what 'psychotronics' *means*."

Michael released a small groan, then promptly apologized. "Sorry. It feels as if I've been like this forever. Do you know what time it is?"

Opal shook her head. "No. It's dark outside, but I don't know the time."

"Menshikov said he'd come back today."

"He told me that too," Opal said.

"He didn't—?" Michael stopped.

Opal, who was still holding him, felt the new tension at once. "He didn't *what*?"

"He didn't mention the Krylov twins?" Michael finished reluctantly.

Opal shook her head. "Who are they?"

"I'm not sure," Michael said. "I think they may be specialists in torture."

Opal held him closer. She was certain he must feel the wild beating of her heart. "He *can't* do anything else to you!"

Michael gave a sharp, coughing laugh, cut short by a wince of pain. "I think this may just be the softening-up."

"But it's pointless torturing you," Opal said loudly for the benefit of the hidden microphones. "You don't know any more than I do about anything he's asked you." There was a subtle change in his body. She dropped her voice. "What? What aren't you telling me?"

"Nothing," Michael said; and she didn't believe him. He pushed down on his trembling legs again and managed to stand erect. Opal let go of him reluctantly.

"There's something," she said sternly. "You can't keep things from me if we're to find a way out of here. We're in this together."

Michael made a small gesture with his head. Opal

moved closer and put her ear to his mouth so he could whisper without his words being picked up by any listening devices. As she did so, there was the sound of a key in the cell door. Opal jerked away from Michael as if she'd been stung, and Michael raised his head in alarm.

A man and woman in their forties were standing in the doorway. Both wore white coats, like doctors, and carried small attaché cases. The man's eyes, behind rimless glasses, were cold as a dead fish. "I am Grigory Krylov," he said softly. His English was overlaid by the distinct hint of an East European accent. "This is my sister, Anna."

"We were just talking about you," Michael said.

32

Danny, the American Embassy, Moscow, 1962

Danny jerked upright, gasping as if he were drowning. He became aware of Fuchsia seated beside him on the bed. "I didn't touch you," she said anxiously. "Honestly." She hesitated, then added, "Can I touch you now?"

"Yes," Danny gasped.

She put an arm around his shoulders. "Breathe," she said. "Deep breaths." Then, as he began to settle down a little, "Are you all right?"

Danny nodded. "Yes. Fine." He drew another stuttering breath. "Fine."

"What happened?"

Danny swung his legs off the bed. "Came back into the body too quickly. Bit overexcited."

"Did you find them? Were they in KGB headquarters?"

"I found Opal," Danny said. "I couldn't find Michael, but if the KGB have her, they've definitely got him as well. Listen—"

"Is she all right?" Fuchsia interrupted.

"Yes, I think so. They have her in a room with a bed, so they obviously don't plan to let her go anytime soon. But there's no sign she's been roughed up or anything. She was actually having a nap when I found her. So I don't think they're in any danger."

"Yet," Fuchsia said.

"Yes, I know. We can't hang around. You happy we go tell somebody in the embassy?"

"That's what I always wanted to do," Fuchsia said. "Shall we go find Mr. Henderson?"

To Danny's surprise, Henderson accepted their story without question. "I'll need to alert the ambassador about this," he said soberly when they'd finished. "This has to be tackled at the highest possible level." Danny and Fuchsia looked at each other as he left the room.

To Danny's even greater surprise, Ambassador Llewellyn E. Thompson took the situation just as seriously as Henderson; but he *did* ask questions—and quite a lot of them.

"This happened outside St. Basil's?"

"Yes, sir."

"You went there together, all four of you?"

"Yes, sir."

"How come they didn't grab you two as well?"

Fuchsia said, "Danny and I went off to look for . . .

to look at the cathedral. When we came back, they were bundling Opal and Michael into the car."

Thompson frowned. "Matter of interest, how did you know it was the KGB?"

"We followed them," Danny said. It was sort of true. To anticipate an obvious question from the ambassador, he added, "They drove very slowly for some reason."

"Arrogant bastards," Thompson muttered. "That's the KGB, all right—think they own the city." He looked at Danny. "And they took them to Lubyanka Square?"

"Yes, sir."

They were together in one of the embassy's meeting rooms, seated around a small, polished table. The young man Henderson was taking notes in a leather-bound book. The ambassador looked as if he might have been on his way to some state function: he was wearing a dinner jacket. All the same, he showed no sign of impatience, which suggested he was treating what they were telling him very seriously indeed. Danny half regretted taking the time to confirm the KGB really were involved: Ambassador Thompson never seemed to doubt it for an instant. Maybe the KGB had grabbed embassy people off the street before.

Ambassador Thompson leaned forward and regarded them soberly. "Okay, now we get to the tricky bit; put the notebook away, Harry."

"Yes, sir." Henderson dropped it into his side pocket, put away his pen, and sat staring ostentatiously into space.

"You kids"—Ambassador Thompson pursed his lips—"that's to say, you two and the two who've been seized, are all in Moscow on a sightseeing trip—right?" He stared at them knowingly and waited.

Danny caught on faster than Fuchsia and said quickly, "Yes. Right."

"Fact that the arrangements were made by a guy who happens to work somewhere in Langley, Virginia, doesn't mean you kids have any connection with any . . . official . . . organization of any sort in that neighborhood, does it?"

"Certainly not," Danny said.

"You're not affiliated with any . . . *company?*"

"No." Danny had been to enough spy movies to know the CIA referred to itself as the Company.

"Okay, now we've got that clear, I'm going to ask you a very important question, and this time, Danny, I want you to answer with the truth. That clear?"

"Yes," Danny said, wondering what was coming.

"Should I worry that anything you kids might be doing could prove embarrassing to the United States if I make a stink with the Russians about the actions of their KGB? I'm not saying I won't take action if you *are* up to something. God knows some"—he coughed—"companies have very young employees these days. I'm just telling you that I need to know, in advance, if there are going to be any repercussions from the Russians when I accuse them of kidnapping innocent American citizens."

"Actually we're British," Fuchsia said, speaking for the first time.

Ambassador Thompson shrugged. "Same difference—we're all on the same side. If need be, I can go through the British embassy."

"I'd rather you handled it yourself, sir," Danny said quickly. Patriotism aside, he knew the Americans had far more clout with the Russians than the British did. Besides, calling on the British embassy would involve explanations and waste time.

"Thought you might," Thompson told him. "Now, answer my question."

"We're not doing anything that could be of any interest to the KGB," Danny said. "Certainly nothing that's going to be any diplomatic embarrassment to the United States." He was fairly sure it was true. They were trying to contact an undercover agent of the CIA, which was admittedly a little iffy, but not about anything that was going to affect the Soviet Union in any way whatsoever.

Ambassador Thompson stood up. "Okay. I'm going

to set the wheels in motion, see if we can't put on a little pressure, find out what the hell they think they're playing at, and get them to release your friends. I want you to wait here. Harry will get you some coffee, sandwiches, anything you need. This shouldn't take long."

In fact it took more than an hour and a half. Danny and Fuchsia began by politely refusing food and ended up eating their way through a plate of doorstop ham-and-mustard sandwiches, washed down by copious mugs of black coffee.

Ambassador Thompson returned looking grim. "You sure there's nothing you're not telling me?" he asked without preliminary as he sat down.

Danny shook his head innocently. "Nothing."

"What about you, young lady? See, the thing is, I'm leaving this posting in August. I don't want to go with a black mark on my record and I'm not sure I trust your friend here."

Good judge of character, Danny thought admiringly, as Fuchsia said, "There's nothing you need to know, Ambassador Thompson."

"Okay," Thompson said, "I'm going to have to believe you." He reached for the coffeepot. "There's good news and bad news."

Danny set down the remainder of his sandwich. "What's happened?"

"I contacted the Soviet foreign office. Protocol. We have to do that first. They knew nothing about any KGB operation aimed against your friends or anybody else staying at the embassy. Didn't know of *any* KGB operation anywhere in Moscow that went down today. But that's not unusual. KGB are a law unto themselves. Most of the time they act first, tell their foreign office afterward, even when it involves foreign nationals. So I told the foreign office *something* had gone down and we were hopping mad, and if they wanted to avoid an international incident they'd better contact their KGB and find out what." He spread his hands and gave the ghost of a grin. "Never does any harm to take a tough line with the Soviets—only thing they ever seem to understand."

"So did they, Mr. Ambassador?" Danny prompted. "Did they get in touch with the KGB?"

"Got back to me after seven minutes—fastest turnaround I've gotten from them in years. The good news is, it *was* the KGB who arrested your friends—"

"That's the *good* news?" Danny muttered.

"The better news is, they're not holding them anymore—they were officially released earlier this evening."

"What's the bad news, Mr. Ambassador?" Fuchsia asked.

"The bad news is, I don't believe the better news. Your friends haven't come back to the embassy, haven't made contact with us since they disappeared. We have no reports of any foreign youngsters wandering the streets. And most of all"—he leaned forward—"our people in the KGB can't find any record of their release . . . *or* their arrest."

"You have *people* in the KGB?" Danny asked, astonished.

"What do we do now, Mr. Ambassador?" Fuchsia asked at the same time.

The ambassador ignored Danny completely as he turned to Fuchsia. "That's the problem, young lady. We'll continue to monitor the situation, of course, but apart from that, I don't see there's very much else we *can* do except hope they find their way back to us in one piece."

33

Michael, Lubyanka Prison, 1962

The woman Anna Krylov folded out the thing that looked like an attaché case into a small table, which she set up almost directly in front of Michael. Her brother, Grigory, opened his attaché case.

Michael felt a chill that had nothing to do with the temperature of his cell. The case contained a collection of shiny surgical instruments, plus several items that would not have looked out of place beside a dentist's chair. With slow deliberation, Grigory began to lay them out on the table.

Anna picked up a scalpel and moved toward Michael.

Opal struck her like a wildcat, howling and clawing. Anna Krylov may have been expecting the attack, for she stepped back calmly. Michael twisted in his chains in time to see Opal clutch her arm, gasping. Blood was seeping between her fingers. Nonetheless she screamed, "Leave him alone! Leave him alone!"

Anna stared at her without expression.

"She doesn't speak," said Grigory.

"I don't care!" Opal shouted. "I don't care if she's deaf, dumb, and blind! I won't let her touch Michael!"

Grigory Krylov finished laying out his instruments, then closed the case and set it on the floor. "She can hear and see perfectly well," he said in his precise voice. "It is only that she does not speak. But you have caused yourself unnecessary pain. She approached your friend only in a preliminary capacity."

The adrenaline rush of the sudden excitement had washed away the worst of Michael's aches, leaving behind a trembling stiffness. He wondered what 'preliminary capacity' meant. The woman had been carrying a scalpel. "Leave her," he croaked to Opal. "You can't stop these people, and I don't want you hurt."

"He is correct." Grigory nodded. "You are not in a position to stop my sister or me. If necessary, we shall restrain you, but I would hope you might restrain yourself."

"I won't let you hurt Michael!" Opal spat.

Grigory Krylov stared at her without expression. "Whether or not Michael is hurt will depend on Michael. How badly Michael is hurt will depend on my sister. She is efficient, but if you attack her while she works, she may cut deeper than she had intended."

It was strange, but Michael felt no particular fear,

perhaps because his body was so numb. What was going to happen was clear. This woman was going to torture him while Opal was forced to watch. The torture on Michael would be physical. The torture on Opal would be emotional and psychological. It would stop only if they gave satisfactory answers to the Krylovs' questions. And the problem, Michael knew, was that there *were* no satisfactory answers. Even if they told the truth, they would not be believed, for the truth was too incredible. He wanted to explain this to Opal, wanted to tell her their position was hopeless, but for the moment his mouth was too dry. He had been given nothing to eat or drink since they hung him here.

Grigory Krylov was still speaking. "Is it your wish that we restrain you?"

Opal seemed slightly calmer. She shook her head. "No." Then the fire blazed freshly in her eyes. "But you mustn't hurt him. He doesn't know anything and he'll tell you what he knows. Just give him the chance. Tell them what they want, Michael."

"You contradict yourself," Krylov told her blankly. "If he knows nothing, then he cannot tell us what he knows. However, your attitude is basically correct. The prisoner must always be given the chance to avoid pain. Thus, when my sister completes the preliminaries, you shall both be questioned and given opportunity to answer."

Opal flared again. "You keep talking about pre-liminaries!" she shouted suddenly. "What are these preliminaries? What do you mean?"

"For the prisoner to understand the nature and intensity of the pain he wishes to avoid, he must first experience it. The preliminaries allow him to do so, although for a shorter duration than might be the case at a later stage."

Opal stared at him, appalled. "I won't let you!" She launched herself forward.

Krylov moved with terrifying speed and, as if choreographed, his sister moved with him. Together, they overpowered Opal in a matter of seconds. Michael could see they secured only her thumbs and ankles with plastic ties. Minimal though it was, these immobilized her completely, and the twins dumped her unceremoniously in one corner. Grigory picked up a scalpel from the table as well, and both he and his sister stood only feet away from Michael, staring at him blankly.

The adrenaline rush had died, and the numbness of his body no longer guarded him against the encroaching fear. His legs gave way again so that he hung from the ceiling chain, watching the twins for movement from beneath his lowered brow. Neither twin moved; they simply stood there with their scalpels. In a moment of useless observation he noticed both were left-handed.

He studied their faces, trying to find evidence of emotion, but there was none. He wondered if their inaction and their passive stares were part of a psychological ploy, meant to frighten and disorient him, or just an indication of some hideous dissociation that left them bereft of any feeling. They were professional torturers. Surely professional torturers could not carry out their job if they had feelings?

Michael found his voice. "Get on with it," he murmured. He thought he heard a sound somewhere near the door, but did not bother to look up.

"What are you waiting for?" Opal shouted. Whether deliberate or not, the psychological pressure was obviously getting to her.

"They are waiting for me to ask you the first set of questions," said a new voice quietly.

Michael's head jerked up. Menshikov was standing in the doorway of the cell. He had exchanged his civilian suit for what Michael took to be the full uniform of a KGB colonel, complete with sidearm holstered at his waist. It made him look older than he had before . . . and far more menacing.

Menshikov caught Michael's eye and gave a grim little smile. "Unfortunately I may have to disappoint them." He turned to the Krylov twins. "You followed correct procedure?"

From the corner of his eye, Michael saw the Krylovs had snapped to attention. "Yes, Comrade Colonel!" Grigory Krylov said stiffly. Michael thought he heard fear in his voice. What sort of man was Colonel Menshikov to frighten monsters like these?

"Then you may stand down," Menshikov said. "These prisoners are scheduled for immediate release."

Immediate release? Michael used the last of his strength to push up on shaky legs so that he could see what was happening. A part of him was suddenly incandescent with relief, but a different, perhaps wiser, part remained suspicious. Was this another psychological ploy—raising hopes only to dash them and thus break a prisoner's spirit? But Grigory Krylov was taking his instruments from the tabletop and placing them back in his attaché case with meticulous care. His sister, stone-faced as ever, let down her scalpel and stood watching him. As he finished and snapped shut the case, she folded the little table again and placed it underneath her arm. Both twins turned together to face Menshikov; made neat, simultaneous salutes; then marched from the cell.

Menshikov unclipped the fastening of his holster to make his sidearm accessible. "I hope you two are not going to give me any trouble," he said menacingly.

Opal asked what Michael wanted to ask but didn't

dare. "Are we really scheduled for release? You're not going to harm us?"

"It is best you are quiet," Menshikov said. He walked over to Michael and began to fumble with the chains. The smell of cheap cologne hung round him like a cloud. "Help me with this," Menshikov called to Opal. He glanced toward her. "Oh, they've tied you, have they?" He turned back to Michael. The ceiling chain suddenly ran free, and Michael collapsed in a heap on the floor. Menshikov knelt to unshackle his wrists and ankles. When he'd done so, he said shortly, "We need to move fast," then walked briskly toward Opal. He pulled a knife from his pocket as he did so, but it was only a penknife.

Michael curled for a moment into a fetal position. Incredibly, the pains he'd endured while chained were a thousand times worse now he'd been freed. Nerves and muscles throughout his body burst into fiery agony as blood circulation returned. But the pain didn't last, and after a moment he tried pushing himself stiffly to his feet. He felt weak, dizzy, and very shaky but managed to retain his balance. From the corner of his eye, he could see Menshikov cut the plastic ties on Opal's wrists and ankles. Were they really about to be released? Somehow he doubted it. All the same, he was grateful to be freed from his chains.

Perhaps that's how he was meant to feel. Perhaps

gratitude encouraged prisoners to answer questions.

"Help him stand," Menshikov told Opal sharply. "Then help him walk. There will be no permanent harm, but for now he will not be able to walk unaided, and it is important we leave here as quickly as possible."

Opal was weeping, whether with relief at being freed or as a reaction to his appearance, Michael did not know. She held him gently, murmuring words of encouragement under her breath, then, glancing briefly at Menshikov, placed Michael's arm around her shoulders. "Can you walk?"

"I think so," Michael said. In fact, much to his surprise, he was feeling a little stronger already.

Menshikov drew his sidearm, a heavy revolver of some sort. "I would ask you to walk in front of me. It is important—very important—that you follow my instructions without question and without hesitation. Should anything unexpected occur, you must stand still, remain silent, and permit me to deal with it. It is absolutely vital that you make no attempt to escape my custody."

Michael almost laughed aloud. The idea that he could somehow make a break for it in his present condition was ridiculous. But he noticed the word *custody*. Despite Menshikov's talk of release, it was obvious they were both still prisoners—and prisoners at gunpoint.

This looked far less like a release than a transfer. But a transfer to where?

The next few minutes were a blur to Michael. The moment he tried to walk, the dizziness returned. He was aware of falling against Opal, of her half carrying him, of wanting to stand and walk by himself, yet not being able. They left the cell where he had hung for what seemed like a lifetime. There were impressions of a brick-red corridor and a linoleum strip beneath his feet. There were doors and guards and the colonel issuing abrupt orders in Russian. While Michael had hung in his cell, he thought he would never feel warm again, but this area of the prison was overheated. As he shuffled forward, using Opal as a crutch, he burst into a sudden sweat as if he'd been stricken by high fever. Then they were outside, and the cold night air of Moscow hit him like a physical blow.

They were not in the square from which he remembered entering the building. Instead they were in a narrow side street. The guards who had escorted them from the jail had disappeared, leaving Opal and himself alone with Colonel Menshikov. The gun trained on them never wavered. Michael stopped and managed to look around. The cold air was clearing his head. The alleyway was ill-lit and deserted. If Menshikov planned to shoot them, he could do it here with little chance of being seen. Then there was a large black car pulling up beside them. The driver got out, a man in a heavy overcoat and fur hat. He walked away without so much as glancing toward them, leaving the car engine running, the driver's door open.

Menshikov jerked open the car's rear door. "Inside," he said tersely.

Michael was too disoriented to speak. "Where are you taking us?" Opal demanded.

"Later," Menshikov snapped, gesturing with his pistol.

Michael half fell, half climbed into the backseat of the car. The heater must have been switched on full blast because the inside was almost tropical. He was aware of Opal beside him and the car door slamming. Menshikov said, "For God's sake, don't do anything stupid." In his confused state, Michael thought he seemed to have lost his Russian accent. Then Menshikov was sliding into the driver's seat, and the car moved off. They emerged from the alley into the city's nighttime traffic, surprisingly a little heavier than he'd noticed during the day. He had no idea where they were, except that after a while they seemed to be driving beside the river.

"Are you all right?" Opal asked.

Michael licked his lips. "Yes," he said, and in many ways it was true. Now he was sitting down, the dizziness had disappeared. His body, arms, and legs still ached, but not nearly so badly as they had done. The warmth of the car seemed to seep into his bones, giving him, little by little, renewed energy.

"Look," Opal whispered. She was gently working the handle of the car door. It was obviously locked. She nodded toward the glass partition that separated the backseat from the driver's compartment, then leaned across to press her lips against his ear. "I bet that's bulletproof glass." Her message was loud and clear. They were still prisoners.

The suspicion was confirmed when Menshikov pulled into the parking lot of a luxury apartment building on the outskirts of the city. They watched from the car as he unlocked a security gate, and tried the car door again while his attention was elsewhere. It remained locked until he returned and opened it from the outside. His sidearm was holstered again, which meant they had an opportunity to break for freedom, but while Michael was feeling stronger now than he had, he knew he was still in no fit state to run. With Opal's hand on his arm, he climbed stiffly from the car and looked around.

"Hurry," Menshikov told them. "It's important you're not seen." He herded them through reinforced glass entrance doors to a silent elevator ride up to a penthouse apartment. The place was luxurious by any standards:

paintwork, furnishings, and curtains all looked brand-new. There was a well-stocked bar in one corner of the carpeted living room. It seemed senior members of the KGB were permitted to stray from their proletarian roots.

Opal guided Michael to a comfortable settee, and he sat down gratefully. Colonel Menshikov closed the door and slipped on a hefty security chain before turning to them. "Okay," he said, "this place is guaranteed free of listening devices, so we can all talk openly. Now I don't know where you kids come from, but there's no record of you here in Russia or back home in Langley or Washington, so I want you to tell me one thing now: just who in hell *are* you?"

[34]

Opal, Colonel Menshikov's
Apartment, Moscow, 1962

Did he say *back home?* Opal stared at the colonel, who was busily shrugging out of his uniform jacket and undoing the neatly knotted tie. The accent was no longer Russian, but neutral, bordering on American. Was this another ploy, another trick to make them lower their defenses? Beside her, Michael moved, triggered a muscle cramp, and groaned as he began to massage his calf vigorously.

Menshikov said, "Listen, Michael, I'm really sorry about the way I had to treat you. No option. What you got was standard procedure. Couldn't deviate or I'd have blown everything—including your chances of getting out of there." He looked at Opal, and his heavy features softened a little, reminding her of someone, although just at the moment she couldn't think of who. "At least I didn't have to give you both the treatment. The manual says pick one or the other, that way there's pressure on the one who's not being ill-treated. Thought the boy would be better able to stand up to it than you, young woman."

"Colonel Menshikov—" Opal began.

"First off, the name's not Menshikov," the man interrupted. He collapsed into an easy chair, his sidearm thrown carelessly on the table beside him. "And you can stop worrying about the fact I'm a colonel in the KGB—that's part of my cover."

"Cover?" Michael echoed. He stopped massaging his leg.

"I'm CIA. As you're supposed to be, according to the embassy. Only I can't find any record of you anywhere. And you two don't even sound like Americans. You're a Brit, aren't you?" He turned his eyes to Michael. "And you're sure as hell not American either. Either Brit or French, I'd guess—you've got an accent I can't place."

"Mali," Michael said. "French is my first language."

"Where's Mali?"

"Africa."

"So you're African, and you're English, and you're both CIA. What about the other two?"

"What other two?" Opal asked quickly.

Menshikov, who said he wasn't Menshikov, sighed deeply and knuckled his eyes. "I suppose I can't blame you after what you've been through. The other two are called Danny Lipman and Fuchsia Benson. But before we start talking about them, let me fill you in on what's been happening, then maybe you'll trust me enough to open up a bit. Hey—can I get either of you anything to eat? Or drink? You can't get Coke in this godforsaken country, but the Russkies do a decent lemonade. I'm assuming neither of you is into vodka."

To Opal's surprise, Michael said at once, "I'd like something to eat. And drink."

"Of course. You've had nothing since they hauled you in. I have salmon in the fridge and caviar, bread, cheese I think, roast beef, and some boiled ham. Any of that appeal to you?"

"Will you make me a ham sandwich?" Michael asked. "Russian lemonade would be fine to drink."

"Nothing for me," Opal said. She still did not trust Menshikov. What he'd done to Michael amounted to serious torture, and she wasn't going to forget it just because he was suddenly coming on all hail-fellow "I'm American." It could be an act. In fact, with every passing moment she was sure it must be an act. But she couldn't blame Michael for asking for food. After what he'd been through, he deserved a banquet.

"I'll make you some tea," Menshikov said. "Something else the Russians do quite well. You'll appreciate that, being a Brit." He pushed himself out of his chair and headed through an open doorway into what was clearly a small kitchen. "Coming right up."

"What do you think?" Michael whispered at once.

"I don't know," Opal told him honestly.

"Do you trust him?"

Opal shook her head. "Definitely not."

"Listen," Michael said, "I'm still a bit stiff. Before he comes back, could you find out if he's locked that door? I mean, he's put on a security chain, but I didn't notice if he locked the door or if it's the sort that locks itself."

"Are you thinking of making a run for it?"

"No, I'm not fit enough yet. I just want to see if he's still treating us as prisoners."

Opal glanced through the open doorway to make sure Menshikov remained distracted in the kitchen, then moved quickly to try the apartment door. "It's not locked," she whispered as she returned to Michael.

"So we're not prisoners?"

"Well . . . ," Opal began uncertainly. Her eye suddenly went to the table beside Menshikov's chair. "Michael, he's left his gun!"

Michael stared at the weapon. After a moment, he said, "Do you think we should grab it?"

Opal glanced toward the kitchen, locked in indecision. "I don't—" But then it was too late. Menshikov was returning, carrying a plate of sandwiches in one hand, a teapot in the other, and a large lemonade bottle tucked under one arm. If ever there was a time to jump him, it was now, Opal thought, but then that moment passed too as he handed her the plate.

"You feed him those until he stops shaking." Menshikov set the teapot on the floor in front of her and handed Michael the lemonade. "I'll get you a cup and a glass."

Menshikov poured himself a measure of vodka when he went to the bar to collect Michael's glass, and took a deep drink as he threw himself back into his chair. "Okay, from the beginning, then let's see if you forgive me, and maybe after that we can get some sensible answers. Like I told you, I'm CIA, working under deep cover as Colonel Menshikov of the KGB. It's a special assignment, short-term and dangerous as hell. Either of you guys read the James Bond books?"

Opal nodded. "Yes." Michael said nothing.

Menshikov grinned. "My assignment's more dangerous, and I've got a very limited time to complete it. Anyway, lucky for you I was on it. I heard you kids had been pulled in. You were the talk of the department. Not often the KGB goes after four American youngsters— I thought you were Americans at that stage—so I started to take an interest. Russkies had info you were CIA. Seemed unlikely to me, but my contact in the embassy confirmed it. I didn't know what was going down—nobody had told me anything; they wouldn't if it wasn't need-to-know—but I knew it had to be important to get you away from Lubyanka before they beat the details out of you. So I assigned myself to your case. One of the perks of being a KGB colonel." He stopped. "You're not drinking your tea."

"Sorry," Opal said. She poured herself a cup of hot, strong tea, looked vainly around for milk and sugar, then decided to drink it black. The first sip was pretty foul. She looked at Menshikov expectantly.

"Thing was," Menshikov said, "there's a standard procedure for interrogating prisoners and bugs in every office and cell to make sure it's carried out." He turned to Michael, who was wolfing the sandwiches, and said with every indication of genuine regret, "I'm sorry about what I did to you, but like I said, I thought it better you than her, and it was the very minimum I could get away with under the rules. Even a colonel can't break them."

The reminder of Michael's treatment sent a wave of anger through Opal. "You turned him over to those ghastly Krylov twins," she snapped accusingly.

Menshikov looked at her soberly. "When the Krylovs go to work, there's no recording made of what happens. That's so the KGB can claim any confession was given freely without torture. Any other time, every word is automatically recorded. I needed to be sure nothing was monitored that would incriminate either of us while I was getting you out of there. As it happened, you were reasonably cooperative, but I couldn't take chances. Frankly, my mission is too important to have my cover blown at this stage. Your problems are just a sideshow." He grinned again, suddenly. "But an interesting sideshow. You ready to tell me what's going on yet?"

Far from it, Opal thought. She realized she was going to be the spokesperson here for a little while—Michael was still concentrating on his sandwiches: poor boy must have been *starving*. "What did you hear about us?" she asked cautiously.

"The KGB arrest documentation said you had information on time travel and psychotronics. Time travel was a new one on me, but the Soviets have been experimenting with psychotronics for a while now and they've always been interested in offbeat stuff like time travel, even if it's nonsense. I figured whatever the KGB had heard about you was probably only half right at most, but half right or all right or not right, you'd still be in for a hard time while they checked it out. What I did to you was nothing, Michael, compared to what would have happened to the two of you if I hadn't taken on your case. And if you *did* know something, they would have gotten it out of you."

"Okay," Opal said. "You've made your point about

that." She still wasn't sure about him, but at least what he was telling them made sense.

Menshikov shrugged. "Like I said, you'd been reported to the KGB as CIA, and when I checked, my embassy contact confirmed it. But it still didn't smell right somehow, so I sent a message to Langley—took time, because it had to be secret and coded and all that jazz. Know what? Langley hasn't heard of you. No records of any of you. No records of a kids' mission to Moscow. So the KGB thinks you're CIA and the U.S. embassy thinks you're CIA, but the CIA doesn't think you're CIA. Weird or what? So I figured maybe you're in some supersecret department of the Company on some supersecret mission—you get a lot of that sort of stuff in the agency these days. Maybe the information the KGB got about your involvement with psychotronics was accurate. Who knows? The Russians believe in it. Heck, maybe you really were carrying secrets about the physics of time travel for all I know. Whatever it was, my bottom line was I needed to get you away from Lubyanka as fast as possible. So I took over your case, interrogated you thoroughly, pretended to have Michael tortured by the Krylovs—there's no evidence to show they *didn't* touch him, and those freaks never speak of their work to anybody—and wrote up a report saying you were innocent of everything. Then I signed the papers for your release, destroyed your arrest records, and brought you here."

He leaned forward suddenly. "Thing is, I went out on a limb for you. I'm happy there'll be no repercussions for me if you lie low and keep quiet, or preferably disappear back where you came from. Which is what you need to do because now that the KGB is on your case, your chances of carrying out a successful mission, whatever it is, are zero. Officially freed or not, they'll pick you up the minute any of you show your faces in Moscow again, even without your arrest records. They'll put tails on you around the clock, and I won't be able to save your butts a second time if you get into trouble. But if you try to push ahead with your mission and you're found out, my Soviet friends won't just grab you so fast it'll make your head spin, they'll also start wondering why I let you go in the first place. I can't afford that sort of attention. So now I need to know what you're really up to, make sure it won't get me into trouble. And in case you're still wondering how much you should say, let me remind you of one thing. You owe me."

Opal glanced at Michael, who was busily picking the last remaining crumbs from his plate. If this man was genuinely CIA, then they did owe him. But how could she be sure? How could she decide if this was anything other than an elaborate setup designed to fool them into telling him everything the KGB wanted to know? She opened her mouth without knowing what she was going to say, and in fact did say, "Colonel Menshikov—" She stopped, then went on, "I can't keep calling you Colonel Menshikov. What's your real name?"

He held up both hands. "Hey, no names! I've gone far enough out on a limb telling you as much as I already have. If you don't like Menshikov, you can use my code name—Agent Cobra."

Opal, Colonel Menshikov's Apartment, 1962

O pal felt herself go cold. It was a setup. Their release . . .
Menshikov's story . . . possibly this whole apartment—all designed to persuade them to open up. And
all of it lies. Menshikov was nothing like Cobra, nothing
like the photographs Mr. Stratford had sent, nothing like
the man they'd seen outside St. Basil's Cathedral. But he
could never have guessed they would know that, so he
had made a fatal slipup.

What to do now?

She threw a quick glance toward Michael. He'd
finished his food, but was still holding his glass of the
Russian lemonade. His face was studiously blank, but
there was no way he could have missed the reference to
Cobra or its implications.

While her mind was still racing, Michael said, "Any
chance of another sandwich, Agent Cobra?"

Menshikov pushed himself back to his feet.

"My, you really *were* hungry."

As he disappeared into the kitchen again, Michael grabbed Opal's hand. "Come on."

Opal stared, fascinated, at the pistol Menshikov had left behind a second time. "Gun or door?" she whispered.

"Door!" Michael whispered back urgently. "I'd rather leave the cowboy stuff to Danny Lipman."

They ran quickly to the door, and Michael carefully released the security chain. Despite the urgency, he moved cautiously so that there was no noise, then, equally quietly, released the lock. In seconds they were in the corridor outside. Without a word, they ran together to the elevator. To Opal's relief, it was already waiting at their floor. "Are you all right?" Opal asked. Although he had moved fast enough, she was still worried about his condition.

Michael pulled open the elevator door. "I'm fine," he said. Then, "Actually, I'm still sore, but I won't slow you down. Come on—he's bound to find we're gone any minute." He pressed the down button on the elevator.

Nothing happened. He pressed it sharply again, then several more times in quick succession. "What's the matter with this thing?"

Opal leaned across him and pressed the button herself. The elevator still did not move. "Are you sure the door's closed properly?"

"Yes." Michael tested the door anyway. Even from where she was standing, Opal could see it was definitely shut. She struck the button again with her closed fist.

"There's something wrong with the stupid thing!" Michael slammed the doors open impatiently. "Come on—there must be stairs."

They came out of the elevator and ran the length of the corridor. It stopped at a dead end. Michael turned. "We can't go back that way," Opal hissed urgently. "He must know we're missing by now."

"The stairs are probably near the elevator," Michael said. "Besides, we don't have any choice."

They ran back, with Opal expecting to meet Menshikov, brandishing his gun, at any second now. There was no sign of a stairwell, but Michael suddenly pushed a door marked лестница in Cyrillic, and there it was. "How did you know?" Opal asked in admiration.

Michael shrugged. "Lucky guess. I thought it looked different from the apartment doors."

Together they began to run down the stairs. Menshikov's apartment was on the fourth floor, but they met no one on the stairway until they reached the ground floor and emerged to find a uniformed guard between them and the entrance doors. Fortunately he was turned away from them, and they pulled quickly back out of sight. Michael indicated they should go back up. Opal followed with some trepidation. Once Menshikov discovered the elevator was broken, the staircase was the next place he would try. But Michael stopped at the first landing. "Let's see if we can find somewhere to hide," he told her quietly. "We can try to get out later when the guard moves on."

"*If* the guard moves on," Opal said.

"I didn't notice him when we were coming in."

It was a good point. Maybe the guard did his rounds of the ground floor, or even the entire building. Maybe it was just bad luck they'd found him between them and their escape route.

There were footsteps on the stairs below them. "Oh God!" Michael murmured. He grabbed her hand, pushed the door, and pulled her out into the second-floor corridor. Opal noticed he had begun to sweat quite badly and wondered if he was feeling as fully recovered as he pretended. But there was nothing she could do about that now. They began to run along the corridor, with Michael pushing every door he came to. None opened. Behind them, someone shouted.

"Here!" Opal said a little breathlessly, and pulled him into a side corridor. Someone was definitely running after them now: she could hear the footsteps clearly.

They got lucky almost right away. The third door Michael tried opened at once. She had the briefest glimpse beyond it before he pulled her inside and slammed it behind them, leaving them in darkness. Opal felt his arms slide around her protectively and held her breath, listening. They were in some sort of storage space for cleaning equipment and supplies. The harsh smell of bleach and chemicals was all around them.

With a wildly thumping heart, Opal heard the running footsteps approach, peak, then fade as their pursuer passed their door. She stifled a sigh of relief, but felt her body relax, and sank gratefully a little more deeply into Michael's arms. He was right. If this was the guard chasing after them, they should be able to retrace their steps and get out of the building before he realized his mistake. She was turning her head to whisper to Michael when the door jerked open.

An involuntary scream died in Opal's throat as Menshikov said, "It's okay to come out now." He glanced around them to take in the storage area and grinned. "Unless you plan to join the cleaning staff." Opal stared at him in horror. He hadn't taken time to put on his uniform jacket or tie, but his pistol was stuck carelessly into the belt of his trousers. Michael gasped something into her ear, and she realized from the sudden trembling of his body that despite his bravado, his reserves of strength had all but given out.

"What is it you want from us, Colonel Menshikov?"

she spat, suddenly more angry than afraid. But she already knew. He wanted them back in his apartment where, she thought, he would drop the charade of being an American agent and return to the methods he'd used at Lubyanka. Except this time, she doubted Michael would be the only one tortured. But they had no choice now except to go with him. Even if Michael was able to run again, Menshikov could cripple him with a single shot.

"Was it something I said?" Menshikov asked as he closed his apartment door behind them. This time he did lock it, using a bunch of keys from his trouser pocket, before he put on the security chain. Then he turned toward them, smiling slightly, one eyebrow raised. When neither of them replied, his expression sobered. "Don't run again until we've sorted things out. This is a high-security building. It wasn't built by the KGB, but it *was* built *for* the KGB. Top brass live here, for the most part. You can't just walk in or out. The elevator won't work unless you do a particular pattern of presses on the start button. There are guards on every floor. They're discreet for the most part, but they're there. The front doors won't open unless you use a key, and they're reinforced bulletproof glass, so you'd need a tank to smash through them. What I'm saying is, you had no chance of getting out on your own and every chance of getting arrested again if I hadn't found you."

Opal said, sullenly, "What happens now, Colonel Menshikov?"

"What happens is I have to figure a way to persuade you to trust me," Menshikov said. "I really thought I was winning until you made a break for it. You going to tell me what spooked you?"

Opal shrugged. There was no reason now why she shouldn't tell him. "You claimed to be Agent Cobra. We know you're not."

Menshikov stared at her for a long time. "How?"

Opal opened her mouth to tell him, then closed it again. The KGB might know all about Cobra, but if they didn't, she certainly wasn't going to be the one to tell them. It occurred to her suddenly that perhaps she shouldn't even have said the little she did say. But it was too late now. "We just know."

"So," Menshikov said, "you're not going to talk." He reached down and withdrew the firearm from his belt. "Maybe this will persuade you."

Opal took an involuntary step toward Michael, instinctively trying to protect him with her body. But Menshikov did not shoot. Instead, he did something entirely unexpected. With a jerk of his wrist he reversed the gun so that he was holding it by the barrel, and pushed it toward Opal. "Okay," he said. "Shoot me."

[36]

Danny, the U.S. Embassy, Moscow, 1962

What are we going to do?" Fuchsia asked as soon as they were alone together. "We can't just not do anything."

Danny shook his head. "We won't just not do anything." Ambassador Thompson had done his best to be reassuring, trying to tell them he was certain their friends would turn up eventually, that it was great news they were no longer in KGB hands, and that the embassy staff were doing everything in their power, yada yada yada, and Danny had bought none of it. He wasn't at all sure the KGB had let Opal and Michael go. Why should they? And he knew the business of the embassy doing everything in its power was so much bull. There were all sorts of diplomatic implications here, and Danny would have bet a pound to a penny Ambassador Thompson wouldn't want to rock the boat too much. After all, as far as he was concerned, the four of them had been foisted on him by the CIA, and he'd no idea what they were really up to. If they got themselves into trouble, he might even want to distance the embassy from the whole business. Despite all the promises of help and cooperation, Danny had the sneaking suspicion they could be on their own. If something was going to be done to help Opal and Michael, they would probably have to do it themselves.

Which was fine, except for one thing. He'd no idea what to do.

"We need to think," Fuchsia said. "Go on, Danny, you're good at that."

She was sort of cute, Danny thought irrelevantly, then dragged his mind back to the problem. After a while he said, "Look, I know I'm always asking you to do things you can't do, but is there any way your time talent can help us here?"

"How?"

"I don't know," Danny said, "but you figured out they went to Lubyanka. Couldn't you do the same now? Look into their future and see where they've ended up?"

Fuchsia stared at him helplessly. "I was watching the car when it took them away so I could see where it would end up. Finding Michael and Opal now isn't that easy. If they were here with us it would be different. I could just look along their time line like I did with the car. But they're not, so I don't have a starting point."

"What about starting at KGB headquarters in Lubyanka Square? We know they were taken there."

"From here? I don't know." She thought about it for a moment, then said hesitantly, "I suppose I might. Outside of a solid time line, space and time are all a bit of a jumble when I do this, so it's not all that easy to find things, but it's easier when I've been to a place for some reason; and I've been to Lubyanka Square."

"Would you try? Just for a moment? Just to humor me?"

They were back in Fuchsia's room and she was perched on the edge of her bed. Now she stretched out, closed her eyes, and gave the peculiar little jerk of her head. A moment later, she opened her eyes again. "Yes."

"You can see it?"

"Yes."

Danny licked his lips. "Okay, this is a long shot. Could you look at KGB headquarters and see if you can find Opal and Michael's time line coming out of it?"

Fuchsia sat up again. "Danny, there are *hundreds* of time lines coming out of KGB headquarters. It could take me *hours* to find the right one."

Danny took a deep breath. "Try," he told her. "Just focus on Opal, or Michael, or both of them if that's any help. Or scan across the time lines until you get a glimpse of them. Or just try to find time lines that sort of look like them."

"You don't know what you're talking about, Danny. Most of it's just not like that."

"You have to try," Danny pleaded. "We're their only hope."

Fuchsia lay down again without another word.

It was the longest five minutes of Danny's life before she opened her eyes again. "That was very, very difficult," she said crossly.

"But did you manage it?"

Fuchsia beamed suddenly. "Yes, I did!" she said. "I know where they went to and I even know where it is because we passed it when we were running from that awful man—I remember it clearly. It's not even very far from here. Shall we tell Ambassador Thompson?"

"Tell him what?" Danny asked. "That you have a weird psychic power that lets you see the future so you can track where people are? I don't think he's going to believe you."

"So we go look for them ourselves?"

Danny nodded.

"I'm not sure that's such a good idea," Fuchsia said flatly.

"Good or not, it's the only idea I have. My feeling is Ambassador Thompson doesn't want to get too far involved in this. I mean, he was happy enough to make inquiries, maybe even send a diplomatic protest if the situation warranted it. But we're not talking James Bond here—he's not about to send in the cavalry to rescue a couple of kids when he doesn't even know what they've been up to."

"It's going to need the cavalry," Fuchsia said soberly. "They were taken away in a big black car by an armed man in uniform. I'm not sure the KGB have let them go at all. I think they've just been taken to some other KGB place where it might be easier to—" She stopped, looking at Danny.

"All the more reason for getting them out as soon as possible," Danny said.

"But *how*? These people are the KGB."

"You only saw one man," Danny said.

"One man with a *gun*! And there may be others at the place he took them—it was some sort of apartment building and there were gates and there might be dozens more KGB inside. How are we going to tackle that, just the two of us?"

Danny took another deep breath. "I'll think of something."

He expected her to argue, but she only said, "Okay, Danny."

It was weird to have somebody trust you that

much—weird and a bit scary. He covered his feelings with an attempt at briskness. "All right, let's go see how the land lies. Maybe we can find some way of getting them free. But you have to appreciate how urgent this is. We don't know what the KGB is doing with them, and even if we get them away tonight, we still have to contact Mr. Stratford and set up another meeting with Cobra."

"Yes, I know all that. So let's get started." She stood up and headed for the door.

Danny stared after her foolishly, then caught himself and ran to follow.

[37]

Opal, Menshikov's Apartment, Moscow, 1962

What are you doing?" Opal asked. She stared at the gun in her hand as if it had just materialized from Mars.

"I'm trying to show you idiots you can trust me. Look—" He walked to the door, unlocked it, removed the security chain, and pushed it ajar. "There. Now you can leave anytime you want. You've got the gun, so I can't stop you. You can walk out of here and find out for yourselves if what I said was true about the guards and getting out of the building. I'll even tell you how to get past them. Any guard stops you, just say you're guests of Colonel Menshikov. Got that? That way, they'll bring you back here or let you out the front door or whatever you want. They'll check with me, of course, but I'll tell them to cooperate. If you do decide to leave, try to get back to the embassy as fast as possible, but remember, you'll be on your own out there."

Opal looked from the gun to the man and back again. If this was a setup, would a real KGB colonel hand over his sidearm and open the door? Somehow she doubted it. But she still couldn't get her head around what was happening, what Menshikov—Cobra?—claimed was happening. "If you're Cobra," she began, then stopped. If he was Cobra, how could he prove it? He'd already handed over his gun and opened the door.

"Opal," Michael said, frowning. "Maybe . . ." He didn't finish, but then, he didn't have to. Menshikov's gesture had obviously thrown him as well.

Opal changed tack. "You can't be Cobra," she said bluntly. "We've seen Cobra."

This time it was Menshikov's turn to look puzzled. "You can't have," he said.

Something clicked over inside Opal's head. Her earlier suspicions had gotten them nowhere. She turned away from Menshikov and set his gun down on the table. If she didn't trust him with some information, they were stuck here, glaring at each other and dancing round suspiciously. Besides, if he really *was* a KGB colonel, what good would the information be to him? Their mission was no threat to the Soviet Union. It concerned something that wouldn't even happen until decades after the Soviet Union finally collapsed. The worst that could happen was that she'd confirm his suspicions they were not what they seemed. But almost certainly he knew that already, and besides, despite what he'd just said, she knew, realistically, there was no way out of here without his cooperation. She glanced quickly at Michael, turned back to Menshikov, and said, "You say you're a CIA operative. So are we. Our mission was to meet up with Cobra. Which we did. Or at least we were about to when we were taken by the KGB. But before that happened, Michael and I got a good look at Cobra, and he's nothing like you."

"How did you know what he looked like?"

Opal hesitated. She knew the real Cobra, whoever he might be, was on an undercover mission of some sort. Which *was* information of use to the KGB. Identifying the real Cobra could be a coup for Menshikov, if he really was Menshikov. She was still hesitating when he said, "There was a photograph among Michael's belongings when he was arrested. You carried an identical picture. Was that the man who was identified to you as Cobra?"

Of course it was. Any fool could have guessed that agents carrying identical pictures must be using them for identification. Opal threw caution to the winds. "Yes."

"The man in the picture is Boris Aleksey Lobanov," Menshikov told her bluntly. "He's a KGB field agent. I know him quite well." He caught her eye and held it.

"Looks like you and your friends were given a bum steer, young lady."

Opal stared. She knew she believed him. He'd produced the Lobanov name without hesitation. What she didn't know, what completely bewildered her, was what was going on here. But all this depended on whether the man in front of her was telling the truth. She believed him, but she was still prey to the nagging doubt that she might be wrong. And suddenly, as she stood there staring at him, she realized there was one way of making sure—and convincing *him* of the truth about *them*. "Listen carefully," she said. "I can understand your reluctance to deal in real names, but I want you to tell me yours. You've trusted us with everything else, so it can't make any difference to you at this stage. If you do tell me your real name and it's what I think it is, then I will tell you something that will prove we're who we say we are as well."

"My name is Carradine," said Cobra without a moment's hesitation.

"You have a son," Opal said. "A little boy named Gary."

Cobra's jaw dropped. "You can't know that. He was only born a week ago. We haven't christened him yet, but my wife wants to call him Gary. The information isn't even on my CIA files."

Opal blinked. Mr. Carradine must be younger than she thought. More to the point, they'd definitely, absolutely, certainly made contact with the real Cobra, here, now, and in this room. She turned to Michael with a smile of relief. He was looking at Cobra, astonished.

Opal turned back. Apart from everything else, this would allow them to complete their mission. "We know that because—and you're going to find this hard to believe—Michael and I are—"

The door of the apartment slammed back with a crash. "All right," a gruff voice said in English. "This is the CIA. We have the building surrounded. Lie down on the floor with your hands above your head!"

[38]

Danny, Moscow, 1962

Danny stared up thoughtfully at the building. It was obviously an apartment building with pretentions of style. Oddly, he was familiar with the architecture, which didn't look Russian at all, but was the sort of thing he'd seen often enough in London during his thieving days. Except that in London the apartments usually had that grubby, seedy look buildings get when they're half a century old, whereas this one looked nearly new. "You sure this is the place?" he asked Fuchsia.

"Definitely," Fuchsia told him. She looked worried. "We can't get in, can we?"

"Wouldn't be too sure about that," Danny murmured. In fact, the security was pretty primitive. There was a high wire-mesh fence around the courtyard that surrounded the building, but there was no electrification or razor wire to stop you climbing it. Heck, there wasn't even barbed wire—probably somebody thought it was too unsightly for the posh inhabitants. The entrance gate was secured by a heavy-duty lock—nothing electronic or coded, no fancy swipe cards or iris recognition or any of those problems. He could probably pick the lock, given a bit of time, although with people coming and going he didn't fancy his chances of not being caught. His best bet, he thought, was to forget the gate altogether and use the big ornamental tree growing at the far end of the parking lot. The dense growth of branches meant he could climb it unseen, and there was an overhang that would give him access to the far side of the fence. He could drop down and be on the ground in seconds.

He doubted the building itself would present too many problems. The front doors might even be open. You'd be surprised how often that happened in an apartment building. Tenants were in too much of a hurry, or just couldn't be bothered, to close them properly. And if they weren't open, there was always some idiot who'd leave a window unlatched on the upper levels. If you weren't afraid of heights—and Danny wasn't— you could always crack in somewhere. The old window latches from the sixties weren't up to much either. You could usually persuade one to open with a credit card and a bit of patience, not that there were many credit cards then—now!—but Danny had brought some neat little gimmicks he could use.

He had only two real worries, and one was guards. You'd never find them in modern London. Minimum wage was far too high and besides, everybody relied on technology for their security: CCTV and all that sort of nonsense. But Soviet Russia was a different kettle of fish. If this was a KGB building—and he strongly suspected it was—armed guards were a real possibility. He hadn't seen any, admittedly, but that didn't mean they weren't there.

His other real worry was Fuchsia. Danny had no doubt at all about his own ability to get into the building, but he wasn't at all sure about taking Fuchsia with him. He wasn't even sure she could climb a tree, let alone follow him up a drainpipe, which was one of the possibilities facing him. Not that he'd *want* her to follow him up a drainpipe. Two people on a wall meant twice the chance of being spotted. At the same time, he didn't want to leave her behind, partly in case some busybody found her, partly because that time line thing she had was proving so useful.

"Fuchsia," he began, then decided on a compromise. If he took her into the courtyard and found someplace where she could hide, he could try his hand at breaking into the building, then come back for her; open a window on the ground floor or something. "How are you at climbing trees?" he finished.

Fuchsia turned out to be very good indeed at

climbing trees. Maybe a bit better than Danny, if he cared to admit it. She didn't balk at dropping down the far side either and landed like a cat. She even murmured, "This is fun, Danny," when he caught her arm to help her with her balance. In fact, she only started to give him trouble when he tried to find somewhere for her to hide. "I'm going with you," she said firmly. "I don't trust you on your own."

"But I don't know how to get inside yet!" Danny hissed. Beyond the fence, a car pulled up, and a couple in evening dress got out. The man looked distinctly the worse for vodka. So did his companion, a pretty, younger woman.

"Can't we just try the front doors?" Fuchsia asked.

"What, ring the bell and say we've come to get our friends? In English?"

"You're doing it again! You know I hate sarcasm. I thought you might pick the lock. They told me at the Project you used to be a cat burglar."

"Used to be a lot of things," Danny growled, "but a nutcase wasn't one of them. Have to be mad to stand picking a lock on a door people use to go in and out all the time. Don't know when you'll be interrupted, do you?"

"Oh," Fuchsia said, abashed. "I hadn't thought of that."

The couple in evening dress were through the gate

and in the courtyard now, heading toward the entrance doors of the apartment building. Danny and Fuchsia were only yards away, but standing in the shade of the overhang so there was little chance of being spotted, especially given the state the couple were in. Danny pulled back a little, then stopped. "Are you game for something really scary?" he whispered.

Fuchsia nodded enthusiastically. "What are we going to do?"

"I want you to keep quiet; don't speak under any circumstances, whatever happens. Just follow me and do as I do."

"I can do that," Fuchsia whispered back.

Danny took her hand and walked boldly toward the entrance doors. They fell in step behind the drunken couple. Through the reinforced glass doors, Danny could see a uniformed doorman. (He hoped it was a doorman and not a military guard.) If the doorman knew the couple, he would open the door. If he didn't, he might ask for ID. In which case Danny planned to find out if Fuchsia could run as well as she could climb. It was just as scary as he'd predicted, but the fear was like the old days when he'd robbed houses, the sort of fear you paid for on a roller-coaster ride.

The doorman recognized the couple! The door was swinging open. And to Danny's horror, he wasn't a doorman but an armed and uniformed guard. But too late to worry now: it was these little problems that made life interesting. He pressed close behind the couple in evening dress, saw the guard snap to attention and salute. He gave the guard a cheery grin and a nod. Out of the corner of his eye, he saw Fuchsia unleash one of her own most dazzling smiles.

In Danny's experience, if you looked relaxed and confident, as if you belonged somewhere, people accepted you at face value. Maybe not Soviet armed guards, admittedly, who were obliged to ask for your papers, but Danny wasn't aiming to look as if he belonged in this building, he was aiming to look as if he belonged with the drunken couple—young guests, maybe even young relatives. If the guard didn't demand ID from the couple, he wasn't about to ask for it from their guests.

The guard stood aside. The couple staggered through. Danny and Fuchsia followed, grinning dementedly. They were so close to the drunken couple now, they were almost bumping into them, but just as Danny had calculated, the couple were in no fit state to notice. In moments they were all out of the foyer and out of sight of the guard.

"Time to split," Danny whispered. "Don't suppose you know exactly where in the building Opal and Michael ended up?"

"Fourth floor," Fuchsia whispered back promptly, and Danny could have kissed her. The girl was incredible.

The couple stopped by an elevator. Since Danny was unwilling to risk riding with them, he pushed the nearest door, gambling that it must be a stairwell. The door was locked.

"Oy," shouted the man in evening dress, then added something in Russian. He was gesturing furiously with broad, angry sweeps of his arm. The woman beside him added a flood of Russian and pointed. Danny's nerve almost broke, and he grabbed Fuchsia's hand to make a run for it. Then he realized the couple were gesturing toward a door on the other side. Presumably they didn't want company in the elevator either. Danny smiled his gratitude and pushed the other door. It opened onto a stairwell.

"Do you know the exact apartment?" Danny asked as they reached the fourth floor.

"Yes," Fuchsia told him. "I can still see a trace of the time line—I'm getting good at this."

"You're getting *brilliant* at it," Danny told her excitedly. "Let's reel them in."

"Just a minute," Fuchsia said, suddenly sober. "What are we going to do when we get there? If they're still with the KGB, we can't very well burst in and threaten to call the police. They *are* the police."

Danny had his own ideas about what they were going to do, but the last thing he wanted was to share them with Fuchsia at the moment. "Whatever about the KGB," he told her carefully, "you said there was just one of them. There are four of us when you count Opal and Michael. Between us, we should be able to overpower him. Especially since we'll have the element of surprise. But before we get into that, all I really want to do is scout around and try to find out exactly what we're facing. There may be some way to look into the apartment. Ventilator shaft or something."

"Okay," Fuchsia said uncertainly.

"Take us to the apartment," Danny said.

He knew something was wrong the moment they reached the door of 289 and found it ajar. Every other door that they'd passed was tight shut. Exactly what you'd expect in Soviet Russia, where trust wasn't exactly thick on the ground. Why was this one open? "Stay back," he whispered to Fuchsia, then moved cautiously forward to listen.

The sound of voices carried clearly, and he recognized one of them as Opal's. The other was unfamiliar to him and the accent was American, which wasn't as it should be at all. Although he couldn't catch many of the words, the conversation seemed to be in English and sounded angry. If Michael was inside, he wasn't speaking.

None of it added up. Opal and Michael had been taken here in a black car by a KGB man, according to Fuchsia. What he was listening to was just Opal and some good old boy who should have been drilling for oil in Texas, not lurking in a Soviet apartment. A sudden, chilling thought occurred to him. What if Fuchsia had got it wrong? She'd be the first to admit she was learning the precog business as she went along. What if she'd missed something, or got confused?

Danny swallowed hard. It was stupid to get paranoid at this stage. She'd said Opal and Michael had been taken to this apartment in this building, and now he was listening to Opal's voice in this apartment in this building. Of course Fuchsia hadn't got it wrong. Michael was in there too; it was just that Michael didn't talk much— Michael never talked much. And the American might even be the Russian KGB man, who'd learned English in America and got himself an American accent in the process.

Actually, the more he thought about it, the more it sounded likely. Chances were, what was inside the apartment was exactly what Fuchsia had predicted: a KGB man who was holding Opal and her strong, silent boyfriend. Just one KGB man. Which meant a rescue was possible.

Before he could talk himself out of it, Danny shoved his hand into his jacket pocket, two fingers pointing forward to create a satisfactory bulge.

"What are you doing?" Fuchsia whispered.

"Pretending I have a gun," Danny told her.

Fuchsia blinked at him, her face a mask of bewilderment. "Why?"

"To get Opal and Michael out of there," Danny said grimly. He pushed the imaginary gun forward in a threatening manner, the way he'd seen cops do in the movies. His heart was beating furiously, but it was a matter of self-confidence. If he convinced himself the bluff would work, then the bluff *would* work.

"You can't threaten people with an imaginary gun!" Fuchsia's voice was rising. "They'll never believe you."

"Yes, they will," Danny told her firmly. He set his jaw. "It's the only way." Women, he thought, never understood these things. He dashed forward, smashed the door in with his foot, and barked gruffly, "All right, this is the CIA. We have the building surrounded. Lie down on the floor with your hands above your head!"

39

Danny, Menshikov's Apartment,
Moscow, 1962

D anny?" Opal's mouth dropped open. "What on earth do you think you're doing?"

Michael *was* with her. He was seated on a couch, looking very much the worse for wear. The man with them (the one with the American accent?) was wearing half a KGB uniform—the jacket was slung over the back of a chair, probably taken off when he was beating up Michael. Incredibly, there was a gun on a table near Opal—a real gun, which had to be a lot more threatening than two fingers jammed into a pocket. "Get the weapon!" Danny shouted excitedly. "We've come to rescue you!" He glared at the KGB man. "You! Down on the floor! I've got a gun trained on your head!" He jerked his pocketed hand. "The CIA has this whole building surrounded. On the floor! *Now!*"

"Ignore him," Opal said to the KGB man. "He doesn't have a gun." She turned back to Danny. "This is

Agent Cobra," she told him.

"Yes, it is," Michael confirmed.

Danny kept his pocket hand—why had Opal *told* him?—pointed at the KGB man who wasn't Agent Cobra, as Opal well knew, because she'd *seen* Agent Cobra; they'd *all* seen Agent Cobra, and he looked nothing like this clown. And what was Opal doing telling a KGB man about Agent Cobra anyway? Their mission was supposed to be a secret.

Fuchsia came up behind him. "Danny, this is silly," she said quietly. "You're going to get yourself killed. He knows you don't have a gun. *Everybody* knows you don't have a gun."

"Of course I have a gun!" Danny said. "You may have formed the mistaken *impression*—" All the same, his hand was wavering. After a long, glaring moment, Danny took his empty hand out of his pocket. Fat chance he ever got to play the hero. He wondered why they were pretending the man with them was Agent Cobra. Perhaps being tortured by the KGB had driven them both mad. As a theory, it made about as much sense as anything else that was happening just now.

Half an hour later, with the apartment door firmly locked and chained, they were seated round the table, all five of them.

"Let's get this straight," Cobra said. "You're telling

me that sometime in twenty years or so I'll be involved in a CIA program of time travel?"

Opal, who was doing most of the talking as usual, nodded. "Yes."

"And I'll do something that will release a plague on America that will wipe out millions?"

"Not just America," Opal said soberly. "We left before it spread fully, but given the speed of modern air travel, you would have to calculate on a worldwide pandemic."

"And you know this because you and your friends here are"—he hesitated fractionally—"time travelers?" Before she could answer, he added, "You have to admit it's not exactly likely."

"Yes," Opal admitted. She had the good sense not to push it further. She'd already given him the pitch, including the personal details Mr. Carradine had supplied. In Danny's experience, it was best to lay things out bluntly, then leave them. The more you tried to convince people, the more resistant they became.

It seemed to work. Cobra said, "You definitely know a lot of things you shouldn't know. I don't mean just for a bunch of kids, I mean for *anybody*. Then you tell me the man who told you this stuff is my own son, the baby born a week ago grown up." He shook his head slowly. "Know what? That's the bit I buy. It's so crazy, nobody in their right mind would make it up."

He straightened his back. "That and a rumor. The Philly Experiment was the talk of the Company at one time, and some people still think we've been playing around with electromagnetic fields and mind control and, yeah, even time travel. So it hangs together. Sort of. So let's say I believe you. For now. What exactly do you want from me?"

"We want you not to send plague samples back from the Middle Ages," Opal said. She thought about it, then added, "Or anywhere else."

"Okay," Cobra said.

Opal blinked. "Okay?"

Cobra shrugged. "Sure. I won't send back any samples. Anything else while you're here?"

Opal said angrily, "Look, you need to take this seriously. People are dying in our time. It was only a matter of hours before the whole—"

"You really haven't thought this through, have you?" Cobra said soberly. "You're asking me to make a pledge about something that only happened a couple of days ago so far as you're concerned, but it's more than twenty years in the future from my perspective. Sure, you're right: from what you told me, there's no way I'd think of sending through those samples now. But that's now. In twenty years I could have information that would change my mind. I could have decided not to believe you. I could have a mental illness that stops me from behaving rationally. Something's not right here. You're trying to tell me an experienced CIA agent—my son, in this case, but that really doesn't matter—would send you back in time to get me to promise not to do something twenty years later? I don't believe that. There's not an agent in the Company who would take that sort of risk—or miss thinking it through, even in an emergency. Which means that part of your story *doesn't* hold together." He pushed his chair back from the table. "Which means I'm not sure I believe any of it."

Danny said quietly, "Your son told me to kill you if I had any suspicion at all you might still send the samples through. He was worried about exactly what you've just been talking about."

Cobra stared at Danny. "How were you supposed to kill me? Shoot me with that imaginary gun you were waving around earlier?"

Danny shook his head. "Poison."

Cobra's expression changed. "What sort?"

"Cyanide."

"He gave you cyanide?"

"Yes."

"Show me."

Danny glanced at the others. "They made me flush it down the toilet," he said sourly.

Cobra kept staring at him intently, his face wooden. "What did it look like?"

"White," Danny said. "Little granular crystals."

"Smell?"

"Almonds." He slipped his hand into his pocket, pulled out the little box, and handed it to Cobra. "I kept it in this."

Cobra opened the box cautiously. His eyebrows raised as he looked inside. "Good God," he said, "the poison ring!" He looked at Danny with a new expression on his face. He took the ring from the box and opened its secret compartment without fumbling or hesitation, then sniffed cautiously at the cavity. "Almonds," he murmured. His eyes returned to Danny. "Looks like you were telling the truth. You really were instructed to kill me." After a moment, a slow, surprising grin began to crawl across his face. Suddenly he laughed aloud. "That's my boy!" he exclaimed. "So it's up to *me* to convince *you*, not the other way around? Now that's *real* CIA thinking!"

"That may not be the only way," Fuchsia said.

Opal and Michael cut in together.

"There was no question of—" Michael began.

"We told him he couldn't possibly murder you," Opal said, glaring at Danny. "That's why we made him flush away the poison."

283

"I'm not offended," Cobra told them. "In fact I'm a bit relieved. The problem is how to convince you." He hesitated thoughtfully. "And myself."

"What do you mean?" Danny asked suspiciously. There was a part of him that had sort of taken to Cobra, but he still didn't really know what to make of him.

Cobra shrugged. "You want the truth? I'm not sure I'd trust myself to make a promise twenty years ahead of time. Besides, there are other considerations."

"What other considerations?" Danny and Opal asked simultaneously.

"Well, the big one is what the hell is going on *here and now*."

"I don't follow that either," Danny told him.

Cobra made an expansive gesture and leaned back in his seat. "From what you told me, somebody set you up. This guy Stratford, to be precise."

"I'm not sure that Mr. Stratford—" Opal began.

"Oh come on!" Cobra cut across her. "Stratford's supposed to be your controller in this time frame. Nobody may have put it to you like that, but it's clear from everything you've said that my boy Gary is your controller in your own time. When you came here, he passed you on to Stratford—standard CIA procedure. I know Stratford slightly, but I didn't know he was—what did you call him? A temporal agent? Anyway, whatever he is,

Stratford gets a briefing on your mission, with instructions to set up a meeting with me. Except he *can't* make contact with me because I'm working deep cover. But he doesn't tell you that. Instead he sends you straight into a KGB trap. That's a setup in my book. The question is, why did he do it?" He looked from one face to the other, a single eyebrow raised.

After a moment, Opal said, "I hadn't thought of that."

"Better think of it now. It could be the real key to your situation. Why would Stratford want you dead?"

Michael sat forward abruptly. "Dead?" he echoed. The surprise in his voice was obvious.

"Sure," Cobra confirmed. "Dead. This wasn't just a mistake, some understandable error in judgment. He didn't get in touch with me *at all*. He sent you straight to the KGB. Stratford knew I was in Moscow, but he didn't know details of my mission. Couldn't know. Didn't *need to know*, understand what I'm saying? He had no idea I was working undercover as a KGB colonel. Far as he was concerned, he was sending you straight to the KGB for KGB questioning on stuff like psychotronics and time travel—both things you know something about, but neither one, I'm betting, you could give any technical details about. I mean, you couldn't say how any of that stuff works. Am I right?"

Opal nodded soberly. "Yes."

"That's a sure recipe for torture. They find out you know something and keep prodding for more. You can't give any more, but they don't know that; and frankly they don't care." He looked at Michael. "What I put you through, Mike, was nothing compared with what the two of you would have gone through if I hadn't intervened. You'd both have been dead inside a week." He looked around and focused on Danny and Fuchsia. "And don't forget, he sent all four of you into the trap. It was only dumb luck you two managed to avoid it."

Michael shifted uncomfortably in his seat. Opal looked stunned. Danny found himself frowning as he tried to take in the implications of what Cobra was saying. "If he wanted us dead, why didn't he kill us all in Langley? Why go to all the trouble of sending us to Moscow?"

"Believe me," Cobra said, "killing somebody isn't as simple as they make out in the movies. Killing four people is a nightmare. Cleaning up afterward, disposing of four bodies . . . We call it *wet work* in the CIA and we have whole teams trained to do it. But Stratford couldn't call in a team, not if this was something personal. He'd have to do all the cleanup himself, and every minute spent on it would increase his chances of being found out. But if he sends you to Moscow, the KGB does all the dirty work for him. Plus he has a built-in cover story. He did what he was asked to do, sent you looking for me, but the KGB got hold of you before he had time to make contact and unfortunately tortured you all to death. Nothing to do with him, he did his job, and you were just a bunch of inexperienced kids anyway."

"Stratford never saw us before we turned up on his doorstep," Danny said. "How could it be something personal?"

"That's what we need to figure out," Cobra said sourly.

40

The Team, Menshikov's Apartment, Moscow, 1962

Does anybody mind if I lie down?" Fuchsia asked.

Danny glanced at her quickly. "You all right?" he asked quietly.

Fuchsia nodded. "Just want to try something." She left the table and headed for the couch. She was small enough to lie flat on it. Danny watched for a moment while she closed her eyes, but the others ignored her.

"What do we do?" Michael asked Cobra. "Go back to Langley and confront Stratford?"

"I can't go anywhere until I complete my mission," Cobra said shortly. "Plague wars may be the big bogey-man in your time, but right now we're worrying about something else." He stopped and looked at them one after another, a strange expression on his face. "Hey, wait a minute. . . ."

"What is it?" Opal asked.

Cobra leaned forward. "You're from the future— right?"

Opal nodded. "We *told* you—"

"You learn history at school?"

"Yes, of course we learn history at school."

Cobra sat back and licked his lips. He looked both excited and wary. After a moment he said cautiously, "This is a long shot, but any of you kids ever hear anything about . . ." He hesitated, shrugged. "Maybe this is nothing, maybe a big deal, but . . . you ever hear anything about a Russian plan to put nuclear warheads into Cuba?"

"Yes, of course," Michael told him. "You're referring to the Cuban Missile Crisis."

Cobra stared at him, then said tightly, "Crisis? You mean they put in the rockets?"

"I think so."

Opal leaned forward slightly. "I'm not sure they got the rockets in, but they certainly started building launch sites. It was all right, though. President Kennedy found out about it and got tough, and the Russians backed down."

"So there wasn't a nuclear war?"

"Oh, no," Opal said. "Nothing like that." She looked at him curiously. "Is this something to do with your mission?"

Cobra nodded. "I was sent to Moscow to check out some intelligence we had about Russian plans for Cuba. What we heard didn't sound likely, and the source wasn't very reliable, but it was too serious to ignore. Put missiles in Cuba, and the risk of nuclear war goes through the roof. You sure they avoided it?"

"We wouldn't be here now if they hadn't," Opal told him cheerfully.

"Does this mean you can leave Moscow now?" Michael asked.

"I'm not sure . . ." Cobra said uncertainly.

Danny decided to put his oar in before the conversation drifted any farther off track. "Listen," he said, "*I'm* not sure we need to go back to Langley. I mean, what Stratford did was awful, but that's nothing to do with our mission. We're here to halt a plague. Stratford may have wanted to stop us doing that for some reason, but he hasn't succeeded. We've still managed to meet up with Cobra. He's sitting here with us now. Mission accomplished, or what?"

"You haven't been listening, Danny." Opal shook her head. "We're trying to find some way all of us can agree Cobra really *won't* send the samples through twenty years from now." She looked at him coldly. "*Without* you feeding him a lethal dose of cyanide."

"I think Fuchsia may be sorting that out now," Danny said.

They all turned to look at Fuchsia. She was stretched out on her back on the couch, eyes shut and eyelids flickering slightly. Twice in succession, her head jerked. After a moment, Opal asked, "What's she doing?"

"My guess is she's checking Cobra's time line," Danny said.

[41]

Fuchsia, in Trance

It was so difficult to explain what this was like, Fuchsia
thought. Even now, when she was getting at least a little used to it, the whole experience was weird. It started
with being able to see with your eyes shut. You sort of
looked *around* them, even though that was impossible.
The light seemed to come in from a different direction,
which she supposed must mean it was coming from a
different *time*. But whatever—if she concentrated, she
could see everybody in the room. Mr. Cobra, looking
puzzled. Danny, dear Danny, looking concerned and
protective and a bit proud. And Opal and Michael, just
looking. Of course, they'd never seen her do this before,
so they were probably wondering what was happening;
but Danny would explain. Actually, Danny was already
starting to explain.

Watching the others was nearly like watching them
with her ordinary sight. Nearly. They were there like

they always were, but even when you concentrated on them really tightly, you were still aware of something stretching out behind them, a sort of multiple image, like the trail a runner leaves behind in one of those open-exposure photographs. That had been really confusing the first time she saw it. She knew where they were stretching into now, of course, which made things easier.

Fuchsia felt her body sink farther into the couch as she shifted to a deeper level of trance. It was for all the world as if she was growing heavier, although she thought she probably wasn't. She was aware she was also stretching, just like the others, but she was getting used to that now as well, so it didn't feel too strange. In fact, it was quite pleasant, as if she'd grown bigger and more powerful.

She entered space-time abruptly, as she always did. It came in like a *whoosh* in her head, and the sensation of expansion was almost overpowering. Suddenly it was as if she was part of the whole universe, stretching into depths of space and eons of time. She remembered what she'd told Danny about looking over a vast plain, and while it was something like that, the description didn't really work. It was more as if she was standing in space and looking around in four dimensions . . . but looking around four dimensions *all at once*. And every now and then she would pick up some little detail, like the building of the pyramids or the meteor that wiped out the dinosaurs or the great crystal battlements of Rigel 5. She could understand what she was seeing perfectly—in many ways it seemed just like an extension of herself—but explaining it to someone afterward was far more difficult. Actually, it was more or less impossible, which was why she hadn't really bothered with Danny. Besides, wonderful though it was, this experience wasn't very useful. (Which, it suddenly occurred to her, was why your mind didn't let you experience it all the time.) To discover useful things, you had to zoom in and focus, find yourself a point of reference.

Fuchsia's point of reference was Mr. Cobra.

She saw him and the start of his personal time line, winding away from the *now* they were all in. It was tempting to look at the time lines of the others—and her own—but she continued to focus on Cobra and pulled back as if she was looking down on him from above so that she could see the whole of his time line flowing into a distant future. As it left his *now* point, it meandered only a very short distance indeed before it began to intertwine with other time lines, generated by friends and family and fellow agents, until it became like a root leading up into the body of an immense, twisted tree, the combined time lines of millions, billions, living on the planet, generating their collective future.

Fuchsia zoomed in and discovered something was wrong.

For a moment she was disoriented. Potential time lines wandered off in all directions, like grayed-out options in a computer menu. These were the time lines Cobra hadn't taken, leading to a thousand different possibilities for his remaining life. She could see the time line he'd been on before they made their present contact with him, snaking its way inevitably to plague and death at Montauk. She could see where it branched—sometime during Opal's description of what had happened—making a new time line, the one they were on now. And she could see where it led. . . .

Except that it led nowhere. Nor did the intertwined time lines that made up most of the tree.

Fuchsia frowned. None of this was making sense to her, which almost certainly meant she was doing something wrong. And that was not surprising, she told herself, because she was very new to all this. What she needed to do was investigate carefully, taking her time, until she understood it properly. What she needed to do was enter Mr. Cobra's time line and find out for herself what was happening. She knew she could do that easily, because the way lay open and he had put up no resistance. She hurled herself toward the *now* of Mr. Cobra, the only possible starting point and her guarantee she would penetrate the right time line.

It was like entering an old black-and-white movie, but one lived rather than just viewed. In an itchy, scratchy way, she *was* Cobra, experiencing his experiences, even catching hints of his feelings. Yet she remained an observer, retaining her own thoughts and feelings, retaining a measure of her perception of space-time, most of all, retaining control. She flew along the time line as Cobra himself (like pressing the fast-forward button!) and saw he did indeed leave Moscow, did indeed return to Langley (briefly), then traveled to his home in New York for a joyful reunion with his wife and baby boy.

The baby was what did it. Fuchsia slowed down her examination so that she could look at the baby and found herself smiling broadly. She liked babies, but that was not the point. *This* baby was Mr. Carradine, still in nappies, far chubbier than he was in later life. This baby was delightful. This baby—

—disappeared in a blinding flash, along with its crib and the apartment and the building and the street outside, throwing Fuchsia violently out of the time line to bounce through other time lines that ended just as horribly, just as abruptly, tossing her like a rowboat in a gale until, disoriented and sickened, she managed to withdraw from the time line tree, pulling back and back until she was once again part of the still, silent depths of space-time, floating like an asteroid in fathomless, star-spangled darkness.

She calmed at once, but became aware of her racing heartbeat as she focused on her body on the couch in the personal *now* of Mr. Cobra's Moscow apartment. The memories of what she'd just experienced were flooding through her, a mix of fire and noise and heat, collapsing buildings, screaming people. She could see the shadow of a woman burned into the concrete surface of a half-collapsed bridge. She could see bodies, most of them barely recognizable. She could hear screaming so pitiful she could scarcely bear the memory. The sky above her head had turned a hideous violet, like some brutal sunset never seen in nature.

Fuchsia pushed the memories away and forced herself to concentrate. She was aware that her body was trembling, aware Danny had risen from his seat at the table and was hurrying toward her, a look of concern on his face. With a gargantuan effort she ripped herself out of the space-time trance and forced her eyes open.

"We're on a time line to a nuclear war," she said.

[42]

Danny, Cobra's Apartment, Moscow, 1962

Cobra said, "You're all from the future, and she can see the future, but the future she's seeing now isn't the future the rest of you remember? Who'd like to explain that to me?" The first gray light of a Moscow dawn was creeping through the window, giving him a haggard look.

"There are different futures, Mr. Cobra," Fuchsia said.

"How can there be different futures? The future's the future."

Fuchsia shook her head. "No, it isn't. Believe me, you have lots of different possible futures, and so have we. The one that actually happens—the main time line— depends on the choices you make and the things you do. I don't understand this any better than you do, but the time line we grew up in, the one where America and Russia *don't* go to war over Cuba, isn't the time line we're in now. In this one there's a nuclear showdown." She hesitated, then added, "And it doesn't turn out very well."

Despite the mess they were all in, Danny was growing to like Cobra more and more. He took things as they came, didn't try to insist they should be some other way. Mr. Carradine had the same characteristic. Cobra was showing it now, for he said lightly, "So I can imagine. How long have we got?"

"To nuclear war?" Fuchsia looked suddenly helpless. "I don't know how to estimate time properly when I'm in that state. My guess would be . . . maybe two weeks."

"But it could be less?"

Fuchsia nodded. "Yes."

Opal said, "I think I know what might be happening here. . . ."

They turned to look at her expectantly. After a moment, Michael said quietly, "Go on."

Opal licked her lips nervously. "Us traveling back in time shouldn't move us onto a different time line. *Couldn't* move us onto a different time line. We know where *our* time line leads because we've already lived through it. So we must *still* be on that time line—"

"Opal, I *saw* a nuclear war," Fuchsia protested.

"Yes, I know. But I think you only saw it because at this point in time, we haven't done whatever it is we need to do to stop it." Opal waited.

It took Danny a minute or two to catch up, but then he got it suddenly. "Hey, cool! You mean *we're* the ones who'll stop the Cuban crisis! If we hadn't gone back in time, Cuba would have led to war. But we *did* go back in time, so something we do now will divert the time line and make it turn out the way my grandfather told me. Wow!"

Danny knew all about the Cuban Missile Crisis from his grandfather, who'd talked about it a lot before the stroke killed him. The old boy had been in the army when it happened, so he'd been really worried that he might be in the front line of a nuclear war. What happened was simple enough. The Russians had decided to teach the Americans manners by setting up nuclear missile sites in Cuba, which was close enough to America for the rockets to hit all the big American cities. Naturally, the Americans were none too pleased. President Kennedy was still alive then and told the Russian premier—Danny couldn't remember his name—to pull the missiles out. The Russians refused. Everybody thought President Kennedy would order a nuclear strike on Russia, Grandpa Stanley said—he *already* had American nuclear missiles in Turkey, close enough to hit all the big Russian cities. But President Kennedy had ordered a naval blockade of Cuba instead, to stop any more military hardware getting through.

That was when it really got scary. The Russians said

they weren't going to remove their missiles and they weren't going to stop their ships sailing for Cuba either. Everybody knew, of course, that if the Americans sank a Russian ship, it was World War III for sure. But in the end, the Russians backed down and pulled their missiles out of Cuba. The Americans took their missiles out of Turkey a few months later, but pretended Cuba had nothing to do it.

Michael frowned. "What's your grandfather got to do with it?"

"Doesn't matter," Danny said. He looked around their faces and grinned. "All we have to do now is figure out what decisions we have to make to divert the time line. Or what actions we have to take, I suppose."

Michael raised an eyebrow. *"All?"*

"Don't knock it," Cobra said. "I'm not sure I buy all of this. I'm not even absolutely sure I buy any of it. But, know what? That doesn't matter. Because the CIA is suspicious that the Soviets are up to something. That's why I've been working undercover. You kids—" He shrugged. "Anyway, let's not waste time going over old ground. If what we do next might make a difference, let's decide what we'd do next if we didn't have this thing hanging over us. Let's decide what we would be doing if Fuchsia hadn't dropped the bomb, no pun intended."

"We would be trying to work out why Jack Stratford

wanted us dead when he couldn't have anything personal against us," Opal reminded him.

"True," Cobra said. He looked from one to the other. "Any ideas, or do you want to jump straight to my opinion?"

"I'll take your opinion," Opal said at once.

"Stratford has to be a Soviet agent. It's the only thing that makes sense. Or a Commie sympathizer, at least. Either way, he's on their side. As regular CIA, it would be easy enough for him to find out I was on an undercover mission related to the information we had about the possibility of Cuban missiles. He wouldn't have details of what I was doing, of course—when you go undercover you work on your own; it's the only safe way—but he'd know enough to warn the Soviets that the CIA was suspicious. Then you all turn up. You tell him what year you're from, and he has to realize that whatever your mission, you're bound to know—from your history books if nothing else—that the Soviets tried to put missiles into Cuba. Worse, you're looking for the agent who's trying to confirm just that very thing. So he has to get rid of you."

"Just a minute," Michael said. "Stratford himself is a time agent. He's bound to know the Soviets didn't succeed in getting missiles into Cuba."

Cobra gave him a withering look. "Yeah, and that's

exactly what he wants to change."

"So now we know Jack Stratford is a traitor," Opal said. "What do we do about it?"

Cobra looked at her for a long minute, then shrugged. "I contact the folks back home and have him arrested on suspicion of treason." He glanced at Fuchsia. "Think that's enough to change our time line?"

Fuchsia frowned back at him. "I don't see how," she said.

"Neither do I," Cobra agreed.

"This is scary," Fuchsia said. "I know we have to do something that will stop a third world war, but I don't know what."

"Are you sure?" Danny asked suddenly. "I mean, can't you go back and look at the grayed-out time lines and see what we did in one of them where the war doesn't happen?"

Fuchsia shivered. "There are millions of them. And I'd have to find exactly the right moment in each one. Like finding five minutes out of your life when you live to be ninety-nine years old. It could take months . . . years. And actually I don't think I could do it at all."

Opal said, "Forget the fancy tricks, Danny. Try to think what we would logically do in these circum-stances. Because we must have done something that made sense logically, otherwise we wouldn't have created the time line we were born in."

"So forget about time lines," Michael said, "and think of what we'd want to do if we just came here on our mission and had reached this stage."

"Well, the first thing we'd do," Opal said, frowning with concentration, "is to tell Cobra about the vials and get him to agree not to send them, and we've done that. Then we'd try to make sure he was going to stay firm for the next twenty years—"

"And we've done that too," Michael interrupted. "By having Fuchsia look at his time line. Which takes it round in a circle because she'd see the business about the war and we'd all start worrying about that. This won't get us anywhere."

"But we can't just sit here and wait to be blown up by an H-bomb!" Opal sounded less angry than desperate.

"What would happen if we simply went home?" Michael asked. "Send the signal and have Mr. Carradine take us back?"

They all looked at him as the implications of his words fell into place.

"Just . . . leave events here to take their course?" Danny asked. "Let the war take place and Cobra be killed?"

"If he's dead in two weeks, he won't send through any viruses," Michael said. He looked over at Cobra.

"No offense, sir. We're just considering all possibilities."

"None taken, son. What you say's kind of interesting, in a gruesome sort of way."

"I don't think I could do it," Opal said. "But it *would* mean we'd completed our mission. . . ."

"Of course you could do it," Cobra told her firmly. "If it was the only possibility. No sense in you hanging around to get killed if you don't have to."

Fuchsia said, "If we go home now, we'll still be on the same time line."

"I don't understand your point, Fuchsia," Michael said.

"If we're still on this time line, we won't exist when we get home. Home won't exist. Because everything will have been wiped out in a nuclear war in 1962. I know this is difficult to understand, because time *is* difficult to understand, but if we signal Mr. Carradine now, it'll be like committing suicide."

"So we can't go home," Opal said, "and we can't think of anything more we need to do here, so . . ."

"Maybe you should stop thinking what *you* should do and start thinking what *we* might do," Cobra said firmly. "Me, I really don't give a damn about your viruses right now. Right now I'm interested in what might be happening in Cuba, because this is my world. And from what the little lady says, you should be interested in that as well, since it's Cuba that'll kill you if you turn around and go home without solving our problem."

"I'm sorry," Opal said at once. "You're right. We can't just look at this from our own point of view."

"So why don't you start by telling me everything you know about missiles in Cuba?"

Opal looked at him. "I think we've already told you everything we know about Cuba. At least I have. You must understand, this is history for everybody here. We only know what we learned at school." She hesitated, then added, "And I'm afraid I wasn't paying much attention."

"Understood," Cobra said. "But let's see how much you really do know between you. By which I mean details. So let's try to piece together what happened in the time you come from. The Russians wanted to put missiles into Cuba, right?"

Michael nodded. "They made an agreement with Mr. Castro, the Cuban president. I don't know the exact terms, but they were going to give aid to Cuba in return for permission to site nuclear missiles there."

"The bit I remember," Fuchsia put in, "was that President Kennedy went on television with spy pictures of Cuban missile sites and loads of Russian military stuff, big trucks and maybe tanks. And he said the Russians had lied about it. And then everybody got worried that the Americans would bomb the Russians and start a world war, or maybe just bomb the Russians in Cuba and start a world war, but what Mr. Kennedy actually did was send his navy to blockade Cuba. And then everybody worried that he'd sink a Russian ship and start a world war, but then Mr. Khrushchev—that was the Russian premier, I remember—Mr. Khrushchev called his ships back. And everybody gave a big sigh of relief." She stared vaguely over Cobra's shoulder. "Mr. Kennedy was awfully handsome. Much better looking than Mr. Khrushchev. Or Mr. Castro."

With the mention of Mr. Castro, something stirred in Danny's mind. He fought to bring it into focus, then remembered the bearded man in battle fatigues who'd attended that weird meeting in KGB headquarters. He'd looked like Castro—Danny had even thought that at the time. Then there was the map of the island with the three names written inside boxes. "Where's San Cristóbal?" he asked. It was the only name of the three he remembered.

"That's in Cuba," Opal said. "I don't think it's the capital, but it's somewhere in Cuba. Isn't it, Michael?"

"Yes, definitely," Michael confirmed. He looked at Danny. "Why do you ask?"

"It was in October," Danny said suddenly.

Cobra rounded on him at once. "What did you say?"

"The Cuban crisis—it was in October," Danny

repeated. "It all came up over two weeks in October; my grandfather told me. This is only the middle of April. October is still six months away. It didn't come up now at all, not in our time." He looked around excitedly. "That's the difference. That's what's different between our time and this time."

Cobra frowned. "You mean the Soviets *aren't* planning Cuban missiles yet?"

"Yes, they are!" Danny shouted. "That's the whole point—they definitely are. I've just figured it out. But these aren't the same plans that led to the crisis in October. These are different plans, with a very different outcome if you let them go ahead. If you let them go ahead, there'll be a nuclear war."

Cobra stared at him without expression. "If we know for sure that they're discussing Cuba now and can give a few details to prove it, leaking that back to the Russians should be enough to make them postpone things for a while until they tighten their security. Which sounds a lot like what you tell me happens in your time frame."

"But we *do* know for sure that they're discussing Cuba now and we *can* give them details to prove it." Danny laughed. "I was at their planning meeting—I saw the maps!"

[43]

The Team, Langley, Virginia, 1962

A cavalcade of police cars, all sirens and flashing blue lights, escorted a Black Maria noisily past Pete's Pies and Coffee.

"That him?" Danny asked through a mouthful of blueberry and apple.

"I expect so," Cobra said.

"Will he get the death penalty?" Opal asked, a little anxiously.

"He might," Cobra said.

"I hope he doesn't." Opal strongly disapproved of capital punishment, even for traitors like Stratford.

"I don't care either way," Cobra told her tiredly. "Stratford seems like small potatoes when you're trying to stop a third world war. Speaking of which . . ."

Fuchsia, who was noisily demolishing a genuine sixties milkshake, put the straw down long enough to smile at him and say, "Quite sure, Mr. Cobra. I've looked and looked, and we're definitely on the right time line now."

"I'm relieved to hear it, young lady," Cobra said, although he'd already heard it several times before.

Danny finished his pie and stared at the empty plate. "You picking up the tab for us?" he asked Cobra.

Cobra nodded. "Least I can do." He looked a different man now he'd abandoned his KGB uniform for a neat suit.

"Think I'll have another piece of pie," Danny said. "Don't seem to make it like this in London."

Michael, who was drinking coffee, said thoughtfully, "I wonder if we'll notice any changes." When the others looked at him quizzically, he added, "After we get back."

"Sure we will," Danny said, waving at the waitress. "No plague. Or at least I'm really hoping it's not there."

"I meant apart from the plague," Michael said.

Frowning, Opal said, "What are you thinking of, Michael?"

Michael stared into his coffee for a moment. "Well, it isn't just the plague, is it? I mean, we're still on the same time line we were on when we left—Fuchsia says she's quite sure of that—but we came back and changed it. The way we traveled in time was like looping the loop. Now we're going back, the exact details can't be the same. There shouldn't be any plague, but will Mr. Carradine remember there ever was a plague? And if he doesn't, where will he think we've been? Remember, Cobra won't even visit the fourteenth century now; Fuchsia's quite sure of that."

Fuchsia put in brightly, "On the old time line it was Stratford who convinced Mr. Cobra about germ warfare. That can't happen now."

"And Fuchsia herself," Michael went on. "When we left, all she had was uncontrolled glimpses of the future. Just glimpses. Now she can see space-time and time lines and things like that. She has more abilities than the rest of us put together."

"Oh, I wouldn't say that," Fuchsia told him modestly.

Danny forked open his new slice of pie. "I suppose Mr. Carradine *will* bring us back . . . ?"

There was a sudden silence before Opal asked, "What do you mean, Danny?"

Danny chewed vigorously, but managed to maintain a thoughtful expression. "Well," he said between mouthfuls, "he sent us off to stop the plague, which we've done. But if the plague never happened, maybe he won't even remember there ever was one, like Michael says. And if he doesn't remember the plague, he won't remember sending us to stop it, so you can hardly expect him to remember to bring us back." He finished his second helping and pushed the plate away with an expression of deep satisfaction.

There was a long silence, then everybody spoke at once.

"Does that mean you're stuck here?" Cobra asked. "Hey, maybe I could get you into the CIA in *this* time!"

"No, that's just silly, Danny," Fuchsia said.

Michael's contribution was a worried, "I doubt very much the changes would extend that far because . . ." He let the sentence trail off as if he couldn't think of a reason.

Opal said, "There may be paradoxes. I don't think you can travel in time without them. I just hope—"

Danny shrugged. "Soon find out. We should be going now, shouldn't we, Opal? Or do I have time for thirds?"

"No, you're right," Opal said. "We should be going."

"Let me get the check," Cobra said. "Then I'll drive you across."

For some reason Mr. Carradine hadn't bothered to explain, the pickup point for their return had to be the same as the area in which they'd found themselves when they first entered 1962. Cobra dropped them by the parkway and they walked the final few hundred yards to the clump of bushes where they had originally emerged. "This is actually a very good spot," Fuchsia remarked. "It's well hidden, so we won't frighten anybody by suddenly disappearing."

"*If* we disappear," said Danny, who'd been going on a bit in the car about Mr. Carradine not remembering.

"Oh, shut up, Danny!" Michael told him, exasperated.

"Who's going to send the signal?" Fuchsia asked. They all had their signal badges, but three were actually redundant: it only needed one to alert Mr. Carradine. He'd handed out the others as a security measure, Fuchsia supposed, in case one or more of them got lost.

"I will," Opal said promptly. She took the badge from her pocket.

"Well, go on, then," Danny urged her. "I want to see if I'm right about Mr. Carradine not remembering."

Opal sent the signal.

[44]

The Team, the Montauk Project, Present Day

The young soldier tried to look stern, but only succeeded in grinning. He showed no hint of plague and was, above all, alive. "Mr. Carradine said I might find you here," he told them. "He wants to see you at once." Then he dropped the formal air and added, "I think you might be in for it."

Opal glanced at the others. Michael was looking around the transportation chamber as if he'd landed in Wonderland. Fuchsia was smiling broadly, probably because Danny had just taken her hand. "Where's Mr. Carradine?" Opal asked the soldier.

"I'm supposed to take you to him if I found you." The grin came back. "Which I did."

If Mr. Carradine wasn't here, who had worked the time gate to bring them back? "You weren't fiddling with the machinery by any chance?" she asked the soldier.

His grin disappeared at once. "Not permitted, miss,"

he told her stiffly. "In fact, I'm supposed to arrest any-body who goes near it without permission. Now, if you'll follow me . . ."

Danny slipped beside her as they fell in behind the soldier. "Looks as if we managed it," he whispered. His eyes were bright and excited.

"I think we must have," Opal agreed cautiously. The corridors were bustling with service personnel, and there was no sign at all of plague. All the same, she could hardly believe it.

But her doubts vanished when the soldier showed them into a familiar office where Mr. Carradine was chatting to a hale and hearty Colonel Saltzman. "Where the hell have you four been?" demanded Mr. Carradine. "Your flight home leaves in a couple of hours."

As the seat-belt sign went off, Opal said, "It was scary the way Mr. Carradine didn't remember anything about what happened." She'd decided things had changed only *after* he triggered the time gate to bring them back, and then everything had switched instantly. If it hadn't worked that way, he would have forgotten before he brought them home, and they'd still be stuck in 1962.

"Well, he wouldn't, would he?" Michael said reason-ably. "It's what we were talking about in the coffee shop. If the plague never got through, nobody died and he wouldn't have any need to send us on the mission." He hesitated. "It was weird seeing Colonel Saltzman again, though. Like he'd come back from the dead."

Opal was thinking about the coffee shop discussion as well. "Do you think we're dealing with a different Mr. Carradine now?"

"Only slightly." Michael didn't seem particularly concerned.

"I'm still not sure about all this," Opal said. "I think we should look out for small inconsistencies—things that are just a little bit different. I know Fuchsia says we're on the same time line, but we've obviously changed it."

Michael shrugged. "Okay." After a moment he added, "Nothing we can do about it if we have."

"No," Opal agreed, "but it would be nice to know." She stared thoughtfully out of the plane window.

After a long moment, Michael said hesitantly, "Opal . . ."

Opal turned back to smile at him. "Yes, Michael?"

"There's something sort of . . . personal I want to ask you about. I tried to talk to Danny about it, but . . ." He trailed off, an embarrassed look on his face.

"What is it?" Opal asked.

Michael took a deep breath and blurted, "I'm an epileptic."

"Yes, I know."

"It's quite well controlled by the drugs I take, but every so often—what did you just say?"

"I said, *Yes, I know.*"

Michael's jaw dropped. "How?" he asked. "How do you know?"

"It was discussed by the team before you joined the Project."

"But I didn't mention it at the medical," Michael protested.

"This was long before your medical," Opal said. "There's a full preliminary check on every operative before they're even approached to join. Any health problems are considered at that stage. The medical is just to confirm nothing new has turned up."

"So I'm not going to be kicked out of the Project?"

Opal looked at him blankly. "What on earth for?" she asked.

With the terrorist threat index at its lowest for nearly seven months, their security restrictions on the plane were relaxed to some degree, but not abandoned altogether. Opal and Michael were seated together in first class. Danny and Fuchsia, to Danny's immense irritation, shared adjacent seats in economy. "I think I'll lodge a diplomatic protest when we're back in London," he muttered darkly.

Fuchsia had her nose in a book. "What was that?" she asked absently.

"Nothing." Danny stared out the window, wondering if the wing might break off.

[Epilogue]

Opal, Manor House Meadows
Nursing Home, Two Years Later

The residents of Manor House Meadows seemed a lot sharper and more fit than the usual population of an old folks' home. Of course, the CIA training might have had something to do with that: all the residents were former agents.

"Bishop to d-seven," Opal murmured. She glanced fondly at the man seated opposite. He had the sort of blue-eyed granite face of Paul Newman. Somehow he'd managed to retain almost all of his hair, although it had turned snow white.

"Could be a mistake," he told her, fingering his rook. She knew better than to take either the remark or the gesture seriously. He was big into psychological chess, using every opportunity to throw her off her game.

Opal moved the bishop and sat back. As he considered his own move, she decided on a little psychological warfare of her own. "Remember the first time we met, Sam?"

"In Moscow? Sure I do. I'm not that senile."

"What was your code name then? Snake-in-the-Grass or something?"

"Cobra," he said. "You know damn well."

Opal hung her head so he wouldn't see the grin. After a moment she looked up again. "Remember when we were in your apartment and I still thought you were Colonel Menshikov?"

He stopped fingering the rook and grunted without taking his eyes off the board.

Opal said thoughtfully, "You handed me your gun and told me to shoot you so I would start to trust you. You remember that too?"

"Like it was yesterday." He tilted his head to one side. "I'll let you take back that move if you want."

"No, thank you," Opal said. "I was wondering . . ."

He looked up. "What were you wondering, Ms. Harrington?"

"I was wondering what you'd have done if I *had* shot you," Opal said. "In the leg or the shoulder or somewhere."

He looked at her for a long time, then gave a slow grin. "Don't be stupid, Opal. You think I'd risk handing you a *loaded* gun?" He picked up the rook again and moved it one square forward.

Opal responded with her king's knight. "So you didn't trust us?"

"Not then."

"When did you decide? Can you remember?"

"To trust you? Course I can. It was when Danny showed me the poison ring." His eyes took on a distant look. "That ring belonged to my grandfather. Passed it down to my father, who passed it on to me. Always knew I'd give it to my own son one day." He reached down to move his queen. "Checkmate," he said.

Author's Note

The stories told in this novel about the Philadelphia Experiment and the Montauk Project reflect two widespread rumors about the secret activities of the United States government. The question is: are they true?

The Philadelphia rumor doesn't seem to be, at least not the way it's told—and there are several different versions circulating. U.S. naval records show the *Eldridge* wasn't even in Philadelphia on May 23, 1944, the day the incident was supposed to have taken place. According to the ship's log, it was on convoy duty at the time, acting as a destroyer escort, and was seen by several other ships.

And when it comes to the Montauk Project, I think we're dealing with pure urban myth. Although I've listened to what purports to be a firsthand account of what happened in an underground base at Montauk, there are too many inconsistencies for it to be believable.

But time travel itself is something else. I am convinced

that time travel is possible, and that there is evidence for its having taken place.

Einstein's relativity theory clearly shows there are circumstances in which time travel can—indeed must—occur. Einstein spelled it out in his famous Twins Paradox.

You begin with identical twins, one of whom joins the crew of a spaceship traveling close to the speed of light. The other twin stays home.

Assume both twins were thirty years of age when they separated. Imagine the space voyage lasted five years. On the ship, the astronaut twin ages five years according to every measure he can apply. But if the spaceship is traveling at 99 percent the speed of light, Einstein's theory of relativity shows that time is moving *seven times slower* on board than it is on the ground. That means the twin who stayed home has aged thirty-five years—he is now sixty-five years old.

In other words, just because the astronaut raced at breakneck speed around the galaxy, he's now thirty years younger than his twin brother. Or put another way, when he lands again, he discovers he has voyaged thirty years into the future so far as life on Earth is concerned. And that, by any reasonable criterion, is time travel.

While time travel to order using marvelous machines

is still well beyond our current technology, there is evidence that spontaneous time travel also can happen. One of the most striking case studies involves a place named Kersey.

Kersey is a charming little English village in the Suffolk countryside. You can see the church tower for miles, and the church itself—first built sometime in the tenth century A.D.—is visible from just about everywhere in the village.

When I visited the place, I found a well-made tarmacadam road running through the village and admired its picturesque stream—locals call it the Water-Splash—spanned by an ornamental footbridge. There is a scattering of thatched cottages, a couple of pleasant pubs and stores. It's one of those places that changes very slowly, and the way it looks today isn't all that different from the way it looked in 1957 when three teenage cadets with HMS *Ganges,* a Royal Navy shore-training establishment at Shotley, were sent off to survey it as part of an orientation exercise.

The survival exercise was carried out over a cold weekend in October. The boys, Cadets William Lang, Michael Crowley, and Ray Baker (all fifteen years old) were assigned to find the village and report back on everything they saw.

They followed a road for a time, then cut across some

fields. Shortly afterward, they came across a gray stone cottage surrounded by large oak trees. A farm laborer pointed them in the direction of Kersey. Ten minutes later, they came in sight of the village. From their vantage point, they could see the roofs of the houses and the high tower of Kersey's church. They also clearly heard the sound of church bells as they left the fields to take the lane down into the village. But as they approached within a hundred yards of the church itself, the bells abruptly stopped.

The church, which had been visible from the fields above the village, was now hidden behind trees growing on the mound on which the building stands. The boys walked in an eerie silence until, turning a corner of the lane, they had their first sight of the village itself. What they saw was quite different from the Kersey of modern times.

The stream was still there, running down the center of the village, but the tarmacadam road was gone, as were most of the houses. In their place was a dirt track with two or three miserable-looking dwellings widely scattered on its left-hand side. There were no houses or cottages at all on the right, just tall forest trees.

The track ran down to the stream, then rose beyond it to the northern end of the village, where there were a few more houses, all of them dirty, small, and old.

The stream was crossed by a bridge, but nothing like the bridge that's there today: it was no more than two wooden planks with four posts and a handrail. The only living things in the place were some motionless ducks on the waters of the stream. There were no parked cars, no telephone lines, no radio aerials—nothing at all, in fact, to suggest a modern lifestyle.

Both village pubs and all but one of Kersey's shops had disappeared. The boys jumped the stream and went to examine the one shop remaining, a butcher's in which skinned ox carcasses were hanging. But the meat was green with age, and the whole place was covered in filthy cobwebs, as if it had been left derelict for months. Other buildings were equally strange. Not one seemed to have furniture, or even curtains.

The boys had the eerie feeling of being watched, although there was not so much as a dog on the street, and their unease increased. Their slow progress up the village street got faster and faster until suddenly they were running for their lives. They turned a corner at the top of the street and stopped, breathless, to look back. Suddenly the church bells chimed, the church itself was clearly visible, the village was repopulated. Normality had returned.

The boys' story was thoroughly investigated by Andrew MacKenzie, then the vice president of the

Society for Psychical Research, London. He concluded that the three boys had somehow traveled back to medieval times, when Kersey was hurriedly abandoned after an outbreak of the Black Death.

Finally, Fuchsia's precognitive talent is a documented phenomenon in the real world—it accounts for some 80 percent of all reported examples of psychic ability. The annals of psychical research provide an almost endless stream of predictive case histories, from the dreams of John Dunne, an engineer who proved capable of seeing the future in his sleep, to the premonitions of dozens of people throughout the British Isles who foresaw the coal-slip disaster at Aberfan, South Wales, that cost the lives of 116 schoolchildren.

Perhaps the most striking and best documented of such case studies involves the sinking of the *Titanic* in 1912, an event accurately predicted fourteen years earlier in a novel called *Futility* by the American author Morgan Robertson. *Futility* told the story of the sinking of a huge ocean liner and contained the following parallels with the real *Titanic* disaster:

In Robertson's novel, the ship was named the *Titan* and was British, just like the *Titanic*. Each ship was approximately eight hundred feet long, with a capacity of three thousand passengers, and set sail in April. While the *Titan* was sailing *from* New York City and the *Titanic* was sailing *to* New York City, both vessels collided at midnight with an iceberg—which struck on the starboard side—and had too few lifeboats to save all passengers.